PADDINGTON'S
STORYBOOK

12/23

PADDINGTON'S STORYBOOK

Michael Bond

Illustrated in color and black and white by

Peggy Fortnum

Houghton Mifflin Company
Boston
1984

A Spot of Decorating, from *More About Paddington*; Paddington Cleans Up, from
Paddington on Top; Paddington Dines Out, Something Nasty in the Kitchen, from
Paddington Helps Out; A Visit to the Bank, from *Paddington Abroad;* A Day By the
Sea, Paddington and the Cold Snap, from *Paddington Marches On*; Paddington and
the Finishing Touch, from *Paddington Goes to Town*; Paddington Steps Out,
from *Paddington at Work*; Paddington and the Christmas Pantomime,
from *Paddington at Large*.

First American edition published in 1984 by Houghton Mifflin Company.
First published in the United Kingdom in 1983.

Printed in the United States of America

Y   10   9   8   7   6   5   4   3   2   1

CONTENTS

1   A Spot of Decorating   *page* 7

2   Paddington Cleans Up   21

3   Paddington Dines Out   37

4   A Visit to the Bank   52

5   A Day by the Sea   66

6   Something Nasty in the Kitchen   83

7   Paddington and the "Finishing Touch"   97

8   Paddington Steps Out   112

9   Paddington and the "Cold Snap"   131

10   Paddington and the Christmas Pantomime   146

Paddington and I first met one Christmas Eve in the toy department of a large London store. I had just missed a bus and was killing time, and he was sitting all alone on a glass shelf waiting for ... well, I suppose he was waiting for someone like me to come along.

He wasn't called Paddington then, of course. That came later; after I'd taken him home and decided to start writing some stories about him. The name seemed to suit him; important sounding, but not pompous, solid and reliable. He was that sort of bear.

The first book, A BEAR CALLED PADDINGTON, was published twenty-five years ago. Since then, there have been many more and I have had letters from children all over the world telling me which was their favourite story. The stories in this collection span the years and are the ones which seem to have inspired, for many different reasons, the most letters.

Michael Bond

February 1983

CHAPTER ONE

A Spot of Decorating

Paddington gave a deep sigh and pulled his hat down over his ears in an effort to keep out the noise. There was such a hullabaloo going on it was difficult to write up the notes in his scrapbook.

The excitement had all started when Mr. and Mrs. Brown and Mrs. Bird received an unexpected invitation to a wedding. Luckily both Jonathan and Judy were out for the day or things might have been far worse. Paddington hadn't been included in the invitation, but he didn't really mind. He didn't like weddings very much — apart from the free cake — and he'd been promised a piece of that whether he went or not.

All the same, he was beginning to wish everyone would hurry up and go. He had a special reason for wanting to be alone that day.

He sighed again, wiped the pen carefully on the back of his paw, and then mopped up some ink blots which somehow or other had found their way on to the table. He was only just in time, for at that moment the door burst open and Mrs. Brown rushed in.

"Ah, there you are, Paddington!" She stopped short in the middle of the room and stared at him. "Why on earth are you wearing your hat indoors?" she asked. "And why is your tongue all blue?"

Paddington stuck out his tongue as far as he could. "It *is* a funny colour," he admitted, squinting down at it with interest. "Perhaps I'm sickening for something!"

"You'll be sickening for something all right if you don't clear up this mess," grumbled Mrs. Bird as she entered. "Just look at it. Bottles of ink. Glue. Bits of paper. My best sewing scissors. Marmalade all over the table runner, and goodness knows what else."

Paddington looked around. It *was* in a bit of a state.

"I've almost finished," he announced. "I've just got to rule a few more lines and things. I've been writing my memories."

Paddington took his scrapbook very seriously and spent many long hours carefully pasting in pictures and writing up his adventures. Since he'd been at the Browns so much had happened it was now more than half full.

"Well, make sure you *do* clear everything up," said Mrs.

Brown, "or we shan't bring you back any cake. Now do take care of yourself. And don't forget — when the baker comes we want two loaves." With that she waved good-bye and followed Mrs. Bird out of the room.

"You know," said Mrs. Bird, as she stepped into the car, "I have a feeling that bear has something up his paw. He seemed most anxious for us to leave."

"Oh, I don't know," said Mrs. Brown. "I don't see what he *can* do. We shan't be away all that long."

"Ah!" replied Mrs. Bird, darkly. "That's as may be. But he's been hanging about on the landing upstairs half the morning. I'm sure he's up to something."

Mr. Brown, who didn't like weddings much either, and was secretly wishing he could stay at home with Paddington, looked over his shoulder as he let in the clutch. "Perhaps I ought to stay as well," he said. "Then I could get on with decorating his new room."

"Now, Henry," said Mrs. Brown, firmly. "You're coming to the wedding and that's that. Paddington will be quite all right by himself. He's a very capable bear. And as for your wanting to get on with decorating his new room...you haven't done a thing towards it for over a fortnight, so I'm sure it can wait another day."

Paddington's new room had become a sore point in the Brown household. It was over two weeks since Mr. Brown had first thought of doing it. So far he had stripped all the old wallpaper from the walls, removed the picture rails, the wood round the doors, the door handle, and everything else that was loose, or that he had made loose, and bought a lot of bright new wallpaper, some whitewash and some paint. There matters had rested.

In the back of the car Mrs. Bird pretended she hadn't heard a thing. An idea had suddenly come into her mind and she was hoping it hadn't entered Paddington's as well; but Mrs. Bird knew the workings of Paddington's mind better than most and she feared the worst. Had she but known, her fears were being realised at that very moment. Paddington was busy scratching out the words "AT A LEWSE END" in his scrapbook and was adding, in large capital letters, the ominous ones: "DECKERATING MY NEW ROOM!"

It was while he'd been writing "AT A LEWSE END" in his scrapbook earlier in the day that the idea had come to him. Paddington had noticed in the past that he often got his

best ideas when he was "at a loose end."

For a long while all his belongings had been packed away ready for the big move to his new room, and he was beginning to get impatient. Every time he wanted anything special he had to undo yards of string and brown paper.

Having underlined the words in red, Paddington cleared everything up, locked his scrapbook carefully in his suitcase, and hurried upstairs. He had several times offered to lend a paw with the decorating, but for some reason or other Mr. Brown had put his foot down on the idea and hadn't even allowed him in the room while work was in progress. Paddington couldn't quite understand why. He was sure he would be very good at it.

The room in question was an old box-room which had been out of use for a number of years, and when he entered it, Paddington found it was even more interesting than he had expected.

He closed the door carefully behind him and sniffed. There was an exciting smell of paint and whitewash in the air. Not only that, but there were some steps, a trestle table, several brushes, a number of rolls of wallpaper, and a big pail of whitewash.

The room had a lovely echo as well, and he spent a long time sitting in the middle of the floor while he was stirring the paint, just listening to his new voice.

There were so many different and interesting things around that it was a job to know what to do first. Eventually Paddington decided on the painting. Choosing one of Mr. Brown's best brushes, he dipped it into the pot of paint and then looked round the room for something to dab it on.

It wasn't until he had been working on the window-frame for several minutes that he began to wish he had started on something else. The brush made his arm ache, and when he tried dipping his paw in the paint pot instead and rubbing it on, more paint seemed to go on to the glass than the wooden part, so that the room became quite dark.

"Perhaps," said Paddington, waving the brush in the air and addressing the room in general, "perhaps if I do the ceiling first with the whitewash I can cover all the drips on the wall with the wallpaper."

But when Paddington started work on the whitewashing he found it was almost as hard as painting. Even by standing on tip-toe at the very top of the steps, he had a job to reach the ceiling. The bucket of whitewash was much too heavy for him to lift, so that he had to come down the steps every time in order to dip the brush in. And when he carried the brush up again, the whitewash ran down his paw and made his fur all matted.

Looking around him, Paddington began to wish he was still "at a loose end." Things were beginning to get in rather a mess again. He felt sure Mrs. Bird would have something to say when she saw it.

It was then that he had a brainwave. Paddington was a resourceful bear and he didn't like being beaten by things. Recently he had become interested in a house which was being built nearby. He had first seen it from the window of his bedroom and since then he'd spent many hours talking to the men and watching while they hoisted their tools and cement up to the top floor by means of a rope and pulley. Once, Mr. Briggs, the foreman, had even taken him up in the bucket too, and had let him lay several bricks.

Now the Browns' house was an old one and in the middle of the ceiling there was a large hook where a big lamp had once hung. Not only that, but in one corner of the room there was a thin coil of rope as well....

Paddington set to work quickly. First he tied one end of the rope to the handle of the bucket. Then he climbed up the steps and passed the other end through the hook in the ceiling. But even so, when he had climbed down again, it still took him a long time to pull the bucket anywhere near the top of the steps. It was full to the brim with whitewash and very heavy, so that he had to stop every few seconds and tie the other end of the rope to the steps for safety.

It was when he undid the rope for the last time that things started to go wrong. As Paddington closed his eyes and leaned back for the final pull he suddenly felt to his surprise as if he was floating on air. It was a most strange feeling. He reached out one foot and waved it around. There was definitely nothing there. He opened one eye and then nearly let go of the rope in astonishment as he saw the bucket of whitewash going past him on its way down.

Suddenly everything seemed to happen at once. Before he could even reach out a paw or shout for help, his head hit the ceiling and there was a clang as the bucket hit the floor.

For a few seconds Paddington clung there, kicking the air and not knowing what to do. Then there was a gurgling sound from below. Looking down, he saw to his horror that all the whitewash was running out of the bucket. He felt the rope begin to move again as the bucket got lighter, and then it shot past him again as he descended to land with a bump in the middle of a sea of whitewash.

Even then his troubles weren't over. As he tried to regain his balance on the slippery floor, he let go of the rope, and with a rushing noise the bucket shot downwards again and landed on top of his head, completely covering him.

Paddington lay on his back in the whitewash for several minutes, trying to get his breath back and wondering what had hit him. When he did sit up and take the bucket off his head he quickly put it back on again. There was whitewash

14

all over the floor, the paint pots had been upset into little rivers of brown and green, and Mr. Brown's decorating cap was floating in one corner of the room. When Paddington saw it he felt very glad he'd left *his* hat downstairs.

One thing was certain — he was going to have a lot of explaining to do. And that was going to be even more difficult than usual, because he couldn't even explain to himself quite what had gone wrong.

It was some while later, when he was sitting on the upturned bucket thinking about things, that the idea of doing the wallpapering came to him. Paddington had a hopeful nature and he believed in looking on the bright side. If he did the wallpapering really well, the others might not even notice the mess he'd made.

Paddington was fairly confident about the wallpapering. Unknown to Mr. Brown, he had often watched him in the past through a crack in the door, and it looked quite simple: All you had to do was to brush some sticky stuff on the back of the paper and then put it on the wall. The high parts weren't too difficult, even for a bear, because you could fold the paper in two and put a broom in the middle where the fold was. Then you simply pushed the broom up and down the wall in case there were any nasty wrinkles.

Paddington felt much more cheerful now he'd thought of the wallpapering. He found some paste already mixed in another bucket, which he put on top of the trestle while he unrolled the paper. It was a little difficult at first because every time he tried to unroll the paper he had to crawl along the trestle pushing it with his paws and the other end

rolled up again and followed behind him. But eventually he managed to get one piece completely covered in paste.

He climbed down off the trestle, carefully avoiding the worst of the whitewash, which by now was beginning to dry in large lumps, and lifted the sheet of wallpaper on to a broom. It was a long sheet of paper, much longer than it had seemed when he was putting the paste on, and somehow or other, as Paddington waved the broom about over his head, it began to wrap itself around him. After a struggle he managed to push his way out and headed in the general direction of a piece of wall. He stood back and surveyed the result. The paper was torn in several places, and there seemed to be a lot of paste on the outside, but Paddington felt quite pleased with himself. He decided to try another piece, then another, running backwards and forwards between the trestle and the walls as fast as his legs could carry him in an effort to get it all finished before the Browns returned.

Some of the pieces didn't quite join, others overlapped, and on most of them there were some very odd-looking patches of paste and whitewash. None of the pieces were as straight as he would have liked, but when he put his head on one side and squinted, Paddington felt the overall effect was quite nice, and he felt very pleased with himself.

It was as he was taking a final look round the room at his handiwork that he noticed something very strange. There was a window, and there was also a fireplace. But there was no longer any sign of a door. Paddington stopped squinting and his eyes grew rounder and rounder. He distinctly remembered there *had* been a door because he had come through it. He blinked at all four walls. It was difficult to see properly because the paint on the window-glass had started to dry and there was hardly any light coming through — but there most definitely wasn't a door!

"I can't understand it," said Mr. Brown as he entered the dining-room. "I've looked everywhere and there's no sign of Paddington. I told you I should have stayed at home with him."

Mrs. Brown looked worried. "Oh dear, I hope nothing's happened to him. It's so unlike him to go out without leaving a note."

"He's not in his room," said Judy.

"Mr. Gruber hasn't seen him either," added Jonathan. "I've just been down to the market and he says he hasn't seen him since they had cocoa together this morning."

"Have *you* seen Paddington anywhere?" asked Mrs. Brown as Mrs. Bird entered, carrying a tray of supper things.

"I don't know about Paddington," said Mrs. Bird. "I've been having enough trouble over the water pipes without missing bears. I think they've got an air lock or something. They've been banging away ever since we came in."

Mr. Brown listened for a moment. "It *does* sound like water pipes," he said. "And yet...it isn't regular enough, somehow." He went outside into the hall. "It's a sort of thumping noise...."

"Crikey!" shouted Jonathan. "Listen...it's someone sending an S.O.S."

Everyone exchanged glances and then, in one voice cried: "Paddington!"

"Mercy me," said Mrs. Bird as they burst through the papered-up door. "There must have been an earthquake or something. And either that's Paddington or it's his ghost!" She pointed towards a small, white figure as it rose from an upturned bucket to greet them.

"I couldn't find the door," said Paddington, plaintively. "I think I must have papered it over when I did the decorating. It was there when I came in. I remember seeing it. So I banged on the floor with a broom handle."

"Gosh!" said Jonathan, admiringly. "What a mess!"

"You... papered... it... over... when... you... did... the... decorating," repeated Mr. Brown. He was a bit slow to grasp things sometimes.

"That's right," said Paddington. "I did it as a surprise." He waved a paw round the room. "I'm afraid it's in a bit of a mess, but it isn't dry yet."

While the idea was slowly sinking into Mr. Brown's mind, Mrs. Bird came to Paddington's rescue. "Now it's not a bit of good holding an inquest," she said. "What's done is done. And if you ask me it's a good thing too. Now perhaps we shall get some proper decorators in to do the job." With that she took hold of Paddington's paw and led him out of the room.

"As for you, young bear — you're going straight into a hot bath before all that plaster and stuff sets hard!"

Mr. Brown looked after the retreating figures of Mrs. Bird and Paddington and then at the long trail of white footprints and pawmarks. "Bears!" he said, bitterly.

Paddington hung about in his room for a long time after his bath and waited until the last possible minute before going downstairs to supper. He had a nasty feeling he was in disgrace. But surprisingly the word "decorating" wasn't mentioned at all that evening.

Even more surprisingly, while he was sitting up in bed drinking his cocoa, several people came to see him and each of them gave him sixpence. It was all very mysterious, but Paddington didn't like to ask why in case they changed their minds.

It was Judy who solved the problem for him when she came in to say good night.

"I expect Mummy and Mrs. Bird gave you sixpence because they don't want Daddy to do any more decorating," she explained. "He always starts things and never finishes them. And I expect Daddy gave you one because he didn't want to finish it anyway. Now they're getting a proper decorator in, so everyone's happy!"

Paddington sipped his cocoa thoughtfully. "Perhaps if I did another room I'd get another one and sixpence," he said.

"Oh, no, you don't," said Judy sternly. "You've done quite enough for one day. If I were you I shouldn't mention the word 'decorating' for a long time to come."

"Perhaps you're right," said Paddington sleepily, as he stretched out his paws. "But I *was* at a loose end."

CHAPTER TWO

Paddington Cleans Up

Paddington peered through the letter-box at number thirty-two Windsor Gardens with a look of surprise on his face.

In point of fact he'd been watching out for the postman, but instead of the blue-grey uniform he'd hoped to see, Mr. Curry, the Browns' next-door neighbour had loomed into view. Mr. Curry looked as if he was in a bad temper. He was never at his best in the morning, but even through the half-open flap it was plain to see he was in an even worse mood than usual. He was shaking a rug over the pavement, and from the cloud of dust surrounding him it looked as though he had been cleaning out his grate and had just had a nasty accident with the ashes.

The expression on his face boded ill for anyone who happened to come within his range of vision, and it was unfortunate that his gaze alighted on the Browns' front door at the very moment when Paddington opened the letter box.

"Bear!" he bellowed. "How dare you spy on me like that? I've a very good mind to report you!"

Paddington let go of the flap as if it had been resting in hot coals, and gazed at the closed door with a very disappointed air indeed. Apart from an occasional catalogue he didn't get many letters, but all the same he always looked forward to seeing the postman arrive, and he felt most aggrieved at being deprived of his morning's treat, especially as he'd been half-expecting a postcard from his Aunt Lucy in Peru. Something she'd said when she'd last written had given him food for thought and he was anxiously awaiting the next instalment.

All the same, he knew better than to get on the wrong side of Mr. Curry, so he decided to forget the matter and pay his daily visit to the nearby market in the Portobello Road instead.

A few minutes later, having taken his shopping basket on wheels from the cupboard under the stairs, he collected Mrs. Bird's shopping list, made sure the coast was clear, and set out on his journey.

Over the years Paddington's basket on wheels had become a familiar sight in the market, and it was often much admired by passers-by. Paddington took great care of it. He'd several times varnished the basketwork, and the wheels were kept so well oiled there was never a squeak. Earlier in the year Mr. Brown had bought him two new tyres, so all in all it still looked as good as new.

After he'd completed Mrs. Bird's shopping, Paddington called in at the bakers for his morning supply of buns. Then he carried on down the Portobello Road in order to visit the antique shop belonging to his friend, Mr. Gruber.

Paddington liked visiting Mr. Gruber. Apart from selling antiques, Mr. Gruber possessed a large number of books, and although no one knew if he'd actually read them all, it certainly seemed as though he must have, for he was a mine of information on almost every subject one could think of.

When he arrived he found Mr. Gruber sitting on the horsehair sofa just inside his shop clutching a particularly large volume.

"You'll never guess what today's book is about, Mr. Brown," he said, holding it up for Paddington to see. "It's called 'Diseases of the Cocoa Bean', and there are over seven hundred and fifty pages."

Paddington's face grew longer and longer as he listened to Mr. Gruber recite from the long list of things that could happen to a cocoa bean before it actually reached the shops. He always rounded off his morning excursions with a visit to his friend, and Mr. Gruber's contribution to the meeting was a never-ending supply of cocoa, which he kept at the ready on a small stove at the back of the shop. It didn't seem possible that this could ever come to an end.

"Perhaps we'd better get some more stocks in, Mr. Gruber," he exclaimed anxiously, when there was a gap in the conversation.

Mr. Gruber smiled. "I don't think there's any risk of our going short yet awhile, Mr. Brown," he replied, as he busied himself at the stove. "But I think it does go to show how we tend to take things for granted. We very rarely get something for nothing in this world."

Paddington looked slightly relieved at Mr. Gruber's reassuring words. All the same, it was noticeable that he sipped his cocoa even more slowly than usual, and when he'd finished he carefully wiped round his mug with the remains of a bun in order to make sure he wasn't letting any go to waste.

Even after he'd said goodbye to Mr. Gruber he still had a very thoughtful expression on his face. In fact, his mind was so far away it wasn't until he rounded a corner leading into Windsor Gardens that he suddenly came back to earth with a bump as he realised that while he'd been in the shop someone had pinned a note to his shopping basket.

It was short and to the point. It said:

YOUR SHOPPING BASKET ON WHEELS IS IN SUCH GOOD CONDITION IT SHOWS YOU HAVE CHARACTER, DRIVE AND AMBITION. THIS MEANS YOU ARE JUST THE KIND OF PERSON WE ARE LOOKING FOR. YOU COULD EARN £100 PER WEEK WITH NO MORE EFFORT THAN IT TAKES TO VISIT THE GROCERS. I WILL BE IN TOUCH SOON WITH FURTHER DETAILS.

It was written in large capital letters and it was signed YOURS TRULY. A WELL-WISHER.

Paddington read the note several times. He could hardly believe his eyes. Only a moment before he'd been racking his brains to think up ways of earning some extra money so that he could buy Mr. Gruber a tin or two of cocoa; and now, out of nowhere, came this strange offer. It couldn't have happened at a better moment, especially as he'd been tempted to break into the savings which he kept in the secret compartment of his suitcase, and which he held in reserve for important occasions, like birthdays and Christmas.

It was hard to believe he could earn so much money simply because he'd kept his shopping basket clean, but before he had a chance to consider the matter he saw a man in a fawn raincoat approaching. The man was carrying a large cardboard box which seemed to contain something heavy, for as he drew near he rested it on Paddington's basket while he paused in order to mop his brow.

He looked Paddington up and down for a moment and then held out his hand. "Just as I thought!" he exclaimed. "It's nice when you have a picture of someone in your mind and they turn out exactly as you expected. I'm glad you got my note. If you don't mind me saying so, sir, you should go far."

Paddington held out his paw in return. "Thank you, Mr. Wisher," he replied. "But I don't think I shall go very far this morning. I'm on my way home." He gave the man a hard stare. Although he was much too polite to say so, he couldn't really return the man's compliments. From the tone of the letter he'd expected someone rather superior, whereas his new acquaintance looked more than a trifle seedy.

Catching sight of Paddington's glance, the man hastily pulled his coat sleeves down over his cuffs. "I must apologise for my appearance," he said. "But I've got rid of...er, I've obtained so many new clients for my vacuum cleaners this morning I don't know whether I'm coming or going. I haven't even had time to go home and change."

"Your *vacuum cleaners!*" exclaimed Paddington in surprise.

The man nodded. "I must say, sir," he continued, "it's your lucky day. It just so happens that you've caught me with my very last one. Until I take delivery of a new batch later on, of course," he added hastily.

Taking a quick glance over his shoulder, he produced a piece of pasteboard, which he held up in front of Paddington's eyes for a fleeting moment before returning it to an inside pocket.

"My card," he announced. "Just to show that all's above board and Sir Garnet like.

"You, too, could become a member of our happy band and make yourself a fortune. Every new member gets, free of charge, our latest model cleaner, *and*... for today only, a list of dos and don'ts for making your very first sale.

"Now," he slapped the box to emphasise his point, "I'm not asking twenty pounds for this very rare privilege. I'm not asking fifteen. I'm not even asking ten. To you, because I like the look of your face, and because I think you're just the sort of bear we are looking for, *two* pounds!"

His voice took on a confidential tone. "If I was to tell you the names of some of the people I've sold cleaners to you probably wouldn't believe me. But I won't bore you with details like that. You're probably asking yourself what you have to do in order to earn all this money, right? Well, I'll tell you.

"You sell this cleaner for four pounds, right? You then buy two more cleaners for two pounds each and sell *them* for four, making twelve pounds in all, right? Then you either keep the money or you buy six more cleaners and sell those. If you work hard you'll make a fortune so fast you won't even have time to get to the bank.

"Another thing you may be asking yourself," he continued, before Paddington had time to say anything, "is why anyone who already has a vacuum cleaner should buy one of ours?"

He gave the box another slap. "Never fear, it's all in here. Ask no questions, tell no lies. With our new cleaner you can suck up anything. Dirt, muck, ashes, soot...pile it all on, anything you like. A flick of the switch and whoosh, it'll disappear in a flash.

"But," he warned, "you'll have to hurry. I've a queue of customers waiting round the next corner."

Paddington needed no second bidding. It wasn't every day such an offer came his way, and he felt sure he would be able to buy an awful lot of cocoa for twelve pounds. Hurrying behind a nearby car he bent down and opened his suitcase.

"Thank you very much," said the man, as Paddington counted out two crisp one pound notes. "Sorry I can't stop, guv, but work calls..."

Paddington had been about to enquire where he could pick up his next lot of cleaners, but before he had a chance to open his mouth the man had disappeared.

For a moment he didn't know what to do. He felt very tempted to take the cleaner straight indoors in order to test it in his bedroom, but he wasn't at all sure Mrs. Bird would approve. In any case, number thirty-two Windsor Gardens was always kept so spotlessly clean there didn't seem much point.

And then, as he reached the end of the road, the matter was suddenly decided for him. Mr. Curry's front door shot open and the Browns' neighbour emerged once again carrying a dustpan and brush.

He glanced at Paddington. "Are you still spying on me, bear?" he growled. "I've told you about it once before this morning."

"Oh, no, Mr. Curry," said Paddington hastily. "I'm not spying on anyone. I've got a job. I'm selling a special new cleaner."

Mr. Curry looked at Paddington uncertainly. "Is this true, bear?" he demanded.

"Oh, yes," said Paddington. "It gets rid of anything. I can give you a free demonstration if you like."

A sly gleam entered Mr. Curry's eyes. "As a matter of fact," he said, "it does so happen that I'm having a spot of bother this morning. I'm not saying I'll buy anything mind, but if you care to clear up the mess I *might* consider it."

Paddington consulted the handwritten list of instructions which was pinned to the box. He could see that Mr. Curry was going to come under the heading of CUSTOMERS – VERY DIFFICULT.

"I think," he announced, as the Browns' neighbour helped him up the step with his basket on wheels, "you're going to need what we call the 'full treatment'."

Mr. Curry gave a snort. "It had better be good, bear," he said. "Otherwise I shall hold you personally responsible."

He led the way into his dining-room and pointed to a large pile of black stuff in the grate. "I've had a bad fall of soot this morning. Probably to do with the noise that goes

29

on next door," he added meaningly.

"My cleaner's very good with soot, Mr. Curry," said Paddington eagerly. "Mr. Wisher mentioned it specially."

"Good," said Mr. Curry. "I'll just go and finish emptying my dustpan and then I'll be back to keep an eye on things."

As the Browns' neighbour disappeared from view Paddington hurriedly set to work. Remembering the advice he'd been given a short while before, he decided to make certain he gave Mr. Curry a very good demonstration indeed.

Grabbing hold of a broom which was standing nearby, he quickly brushed the soot into a large pile in the middle of the hearth. Then he poked the broom up the chimney and waved it around several times. His hopes were speedily realised. There was a rushing sound and a moment later an even bigger load of soot landed at his feet. Ignoring the black clouds which were beginning to fill the room, Paddington removed the cardboard box from his basket, and examined Mrs. Bird's shopping. As he'd feared, some of it had suffered rather badly under the weight and he added the remains of some broken custard tarts, several squashed tomatoes, and a number of cracked eggs to the pile.

It was while he was stirring it all up with the handle of the broom that Mr. Curry came back into the room. For a moment he stood as if transfixed.

"Bear!" he bellowed. "Bear! What on earth do you think you're doing?"

Paddington stood up and gazed at his handiwork. Now that he was viewing it from a distance he had to admit it *was* rather worse than he had intended.

"It's all part of my demonstration, Mr. Curry," he explained, with more confidence than he felt.

"Now," he said, putting on his best salesman's voice as he consulted the instructions again, "I'm sure you will agree that no ordinary cleaner would be any good with this mess."

For once in his life it seemed that Mr. Curry was in complete and utter accord with Paddington. "Have you taken leave of your senses, bear?" he spluttered.

Paddington gave the cardboard box a slap. "No, Mr. Curry," he exclaimed. "Never fear, it's all in here. Ask no questions, I'll tell no lies."

Mr. Curry looked as if there were a good many questions he was only too eager to ask, but instead he pointed a trembling finger at the box.

"Never fear, it's all in here!" he bellowed. "It had better all be in there! If it's not all in there within thirty seconds I shall..."

Mr. Curry paused for breath, suddenly at a loss for words.

Taking advantage of the moment, Paddington opened the lid of the box and withdrew a long piece of wire with a plug on the end.

He peered at the skirting board. "Can you tell me where your socket is, Mr. Curry?" he enquired.

If Paddington had asked the Browns' neighbour for the loan of a million pounds he couldn't have had a more unfavourable reaction. Mr. Curry's face, which had been growing redder and redder with rage, suddenly went a deep shade of purple as he gazed at the object in Paddington's paw.

"My socket?" he roared. "*My socket?* I haven't any sockets, bear! I don't even have any electricity. I use gas!"

Paddington's jaw dropped, and the plug slipped from his paw and fell unheeded to the floor as he gazed at the Browns' neighbour. If Mr. Curry's face had gone a deep shade of purple, Paddington's — or the little that could be seen of it beneath his fur — was as white as a sheet.

He wasn't sure what happened next. He remembered Mr. Curry picking up the cardboard box as if he was about to hurl it through the window, but he didn't wait to see any more. He dashed out through the front door and back into number thirty-two Windsor Gardens as if his very life depended on it.

To his surprise the door was already open, but it wasn't until he cannoned into Mr. Gruber that he discovered the reason why. His friend was deep in conversation with the other members of the family.

For some reason they seemed even more pleased to see him than he was to see them.

"There you are!" exclaimed Mrs. Bird.

"Thank goodness," said Mrs. Brown thankfully.

"Are you all right?" chorused Jonathan and Judy.

"I think so," gasped Paddington, peering over his shoulder as he hastily closed the door behind him.

"No one's tried to sell you a vacuum cleaner?" asked Mrs. Bird.

Paddington stared at the Browns' housekeeper in amazement. It really was uncanny the way Mrs. Bird 'knew' about things.

"There have been some 'goings-on' down at the market this morning, Mr. Brown," broke in Mr. Gruber. "That's why I popped in. Someone's been selling dud vacuum cleaners and when I heard you'd been seen talking to him I began to get worried."

"When you were so late back we thought something might have happened to you," said Mrs. Brown.

"Well," said Paddington vaguely, "I think it has!"

Paddington launched into his explanations. It was a bit difficult, partly because he wasn't too sure how to put some of it into words, but also because there was a good deal of noise going on outside. Shouts and bangs, and the sound of a loud argument, followed a moment or so later by the roar of a car drawing away.

"Fancy trying to take advantage of someone like that," said Mrs. Bird grimly, when Paddington had finished.

"He seemed quite a nice man, Mrs. Bird," said Paddington.

"I didn't mean the vacuum cleaner salesman," said Mrs. Bird. "At least he gave you *something* for your money — even if it didn't work. I meant Mr. Curry. He's always after something for nothing."

"He's too mean to get his chimney swept for a start," said Judy.

"And I bet he's still waiting to see if electricity catches on before he changes over," agreed Jonathan.

34

They broke off as the telephone started to ring and Mrs. Bird hurried across the hall to answer it.

' "Yes," she said after a moment. "Really? Yes, of course. Well, we'll do our best," she added after a while, "but it may not be for some time. Probably later on this morning."

The others grew more and more mystified as they listened to their end of the conversation.

"What on earth was all that about?" asked Mrs. Brown, as her housekeeper replaced the receiver.

"It seems," said Mrs. Bird gravely, "that the police think they may have caught the man who's been selling the dud vacuum cleaners. They want someone to go down and identify him."

"Oh, dear," said Mrs. Brown. "I don't really like the idea of Paddington being involved in things like that."

"Who said anything about Paddington?" asked Mrs. Bird innocently. "Anyway, I suggest we all have a nice hot drink before we do anything else. There's no point in rushing things."

The others exchanged glances as they followed Mrs. Bird into the kitchen. She could be very infuriating at times. But the Browns' housekeeper refused to be drawn, and it wasn't until they were all settled round the kitchen table with their second lot of elevenses that she brought the matter up again.

"It seems," she mused, "that the man they arrested was caught right outside our house. He was carrying a cleaner at the time. He said his name was Murray, or Hurry or something like that... Anyway, he insists we know him."

"Crumbs!" exclaimed Jonathan as light began to dawn. "Don't say they picked on Mr. Curry by mistake!"

"I bet that's what all the row was about just now," said Judy. "I bet he was coming round here to complain!"

"Which is why," said Mrs. Bird, when all the excitement had died down, "I really think it might be better if Paddington doesn't go down to the Police station. It might be rubbing salt into the wound."

"I quite agree," said Mr. Gruber. "In fact while you're gone perhaps young Mr. Brown and I can go next door and clear up some of the mess."

"Bags we help too," said Jonathan and Judy eagerly.

All eyes turned to Paddington, who was savouring his drink with even more relish than usual. What with Mr. Gruber's book on diseases and the disastrous events in Mr. Curry's house he'd almost begun to wonder if he would ever have any elevenses again.

"I think," he announced, as he clasped the mug firmly between his paws, "I shall never take my cocoa for granted again!"

CHAPTER THREE

Paddington Dines Out

"I vote," said Mr. Brown, "that we celebrate the occasion by visiting a restaurant. All those in favour say 'aye'."

Mr. Brown's suggestion had a mixed reception. Jonathan and Judy called out "aye" at once. Mrs. Brown looked rather doubtful and Mrs. Bird kept her eyes firmly on her knitting.

"Do you think it wise, Henry?" said Mrs. Brown. "You know what Paddington's like when we take him out. Things happen."

"It *is* his birthday," replied Mr. Brown.

"And his anniversary," said Judy. "Sort of."

The Browns were holding a council of war. It was

Paddington's summer birthday. Being a bear, Paddington had two birthdays every year — one at Christmas and the other in mid-summer. That apart, he had now been with the Browns for a little over a year and it had been decided to celebrate the two occasions at the same time.

"After all, we ought to do *something*," said Mr. Brown, playing his trump card. "If we hadn't seen him that day on Paddington station we might never have met him and goodness knows where he would have ended up."

The Browns were silent for a moment as they considered the awful possibility of never having met Paddington.

"I must say," remarked Mrs. Bird, in a voice which really decided the matter, "the house wouldn't be the same without him."

"That settles it," said Mr. Brown. "I'll ring the Porchester right away and reserve a table for tonight."

"Oh, Henry," exclaimed Mrs. Brown. "Not the *Porchester*. That's such an expensive place."

Mr. Brown waved his hand in the air. "Nothing but the best is good enough for Paddington," he said generously. "We'll invite Mr. Gruber as well and make a real party of it."

"By the way," he continued, "where *is* Paddington? I haven't seen him for ages."

"He was peering through the letter-box just now," said Mrs. Bird. "I think he was looking for the postman."

Paddington liked birthdays. He didn't get many letters — only his catalogues and an occasional postcard from his

Aunt Lucy in Peru — but today the mantelpiece in the dining-room was already filled to over-flowing with cards and he was looking forward to some more arriving. There had been a card from each of the Browns, one from Mr. Gruber, and quite a surprising number from various people who lived in the neighbourhood. There was even an old one from Mr. Curry, which Mrs. Bird recognised as one Paddington had sent him the year before, but she had wisely decided not to point this out.

Then there were all the parcels. Paddington was very keen on parcels — especially when they were well wrapped up with plenty of paper and string. In fact he had done extremely well for himself, and the news that they were all

going out that evening as well came as a great surprise.

"Mind you," said Mrs. Brown, "you'll have to have a bath first."

"A bath!" exclaimed Paddington. "On my birthday?"

Paddington looked most upset at the thought of having a bath on his birthday.

"The Porchester is a very famous restaurant," explained Mrs. Brown. "Only the best people go there."

And, despite his protests, he was sent upstairs that afternoon with a bath cube and some soap and strict instructions not to come down again until he was clean.

Excitement in the Browns' house mounted during the afternoon and by the time Mr. Gruber arrived, looking rather self-conscious in an evening-dress suit which he hadn't worn for many years, it had reached fever pitch.

"I don't think I've ever been to the Porchester before, Mr. Brown," he whispered to Paddington in the hall. "So that makes two of us. It'll be a nice change from cocoa and buns."

Paddington became more and more excited on the journey to the restaurant. He always enjoyed seeing the lights of London and even though it was summer quite a few of them had already come on by the time they got there.

He followed Mr. Brown up the steps of the restaurant and in through some large doors, giving the man who held them open a friendly wave of his paw.

In the distance there was the sound of music and as they all gathered inside the entrance in order to leave their coats at the cloakroom, Paddington looked around with interest at the chandeliers hanging from the ceiling and at the dozens of waiters gliding to and fro.

"Here comes the head waiter," said Mr. Brown, as a tall, superior-looking man approached. "We've booked a table near the orchestra," he called. "In the name of Brown."

The head waiter stared at Paddington. "Is the young ...er...bear gentleman with you?" he asked, looking down his nose.

"With us?" said Mr. Brown. "We're with *him*. It's his party."

"Oh," said the man disapprovingly. "Then I'm afraid you can't come in."

"What!" exclaimed Paddington amid a chorus of dismay. "But I went without a second helping at lunch specially."

"I'm afraid the young gentlemen isn't wearing evening dress," explained the man. "Everyone at the Porchester has to wear evening dress."

Paddington could hardly believe his ears and he gave the man a hard stare.

41

"Bears don't have evening dress," said Judy, squeezing his paw. "They have evening fur — and Paddington's has been washed specially."

The head waiter looked at Paddington doubtfully. Paddington had a very persistent stare when he liked, and some of the special ones his Aunt Lucy had taught him were very powerful indeed. He coughed. "I daresay," he said, "we might make an exception — just this once."

He turned and led the way through the crowded restaurant, past tables covered with snowy white cloths and gleaming silver, towards a big round table near the orchestra. Paddington followed on close behind and by the time they reached it the man's neck had gone a funny shade of red.

When they were all seated the head waiter gave them each a huge card on which was printed a list of all the dishes. Paddington had to hold his with both paws and he stared at it in amazement.

"Well, Paddington," said Mr. Brown. "What would you like to start with? Soup? Hors d'œuvre?"

Paddington looked at his menu in disgust. He didn't think much of it at all. "I don't know what I would like, Mr. Brown," he said. "My programme's full of mistakes and I can't read it."

"*Mistakes!*" The head waiter raised one eyebrow to its full height and looked at Paddington severely. "There is never a mistake on a Porchester menu."

"These aren't mistakes, Paddington," whispered Judy, as she looked over his shoulder. "It's French."

"French!" exclaimed Paddington. "Fancy printing a menu in French!"

Mr. Brown hastily scanned his own card. "Er...have you anything suitable for a young bear's treat?" he asked.

"A young bear's treat?" repeated the head waiter haughtily. "We pride ourselves that there is nothing one cannot obtain at the Porchester."

"In that case," said Paddington, looking most relieved, "I think I'll have a marmalade sandwich."

Looking around, Paddington decided a place as important as the Porchester must serve very good marmalade sandwiches, and he was anxious to test one.

"I beg your pardon, sir?" exclaimed the waiter. "Did you say a marmalade sandwich?"

"Yes, please," said Paddington. "With custard."

"For dinner?" said the man.

"Yes," said Paddington firmly. "I'm very fond of marmalade and you said there was nothing you don't have."

The man swallowed hard. In all his years at the Porchester he'd never been asked for a marmalade sandwich before, particularly by a bear. He beckoned to another waiter standing nearby. "A marmalade sandwich for the young bear gentleman," he said. "With custard."

"A marmalade sandwich for the young bear gentleman — with custard," repeated the second waiter. He disappeared through a door leading to the kitchens as if in a dream and the Browns heard the order repeated several more times before it closed. They looked around uneasily while they gave another waiter their own orders.

There seemed to be some sort of commotion going on in the kitchen. Several times they heard raised voices and once the door opened and a man in a chef's hat appeared round the corner and stared in their direction.

"Perhaps, sir," said yet another waiter, as he wheeled a huge trolley laden with dishes towards the table, "would you care for some hors d'œuvre while you wait?"

"That's a sort of salad," Mr. Brown explained to Paddington.

Paddington licked his whiskers. "It looks a very good bargain," he said, staring at all the dishes. "I think perhaps I will."

"Oh, dear," said Mrs. Brown, as Paddington began helping himself. "You're not supposed to eat it *from* the trolley, Paddington."

Paddington looked most disappointed as he watched the waiter serve the hors d'œuvre. It wasn't really quite such good value as he'd thought. But by the time the man had finished piling his plate with vegetables and pickles, salad, and a pile of interesting looking little silver onions he began to change his mind again. Perhaps, he decided, he couldn't have managed the whole trolleyful after all.

While Mr. Brown gave the rest of the orders — soup for the others followed by fish and a special omelet for Mr. Gruber — Paddington sat back and prepared to enjoy himself.

"Would you like anything to drink, Paddington?" asked Mr. Brown.

"No, thank you, Mr. Brown," said Paddington. "I have a bowl of water."

"I don't think that's drinking water, Mr. Brown," said Mr. Gruber tactfully. "That's to dip your paws in when they get sticky. That's what's known as a paw bowl."

"A paw bowl?" exclaimed Paddington. "But I had a bath this afternoon."

"Never mind," said Mr. Brown hastily. "I'll send for the lemonade waiter — then you can have an orange squash or something."

Paddington was getting more and more confused. It was all most complicated and he'd never seen so many waiters before. He decided to concentrate on eating for a bit.

"Most enjoyable," said Mr. Gruber a few minutes later when he had finished his soup. "I shall look forward to my omelet now." He looked across the table at Paddington. "Are you enjoying your hors d'oeuvre, Mr. Brown?"

"It's very nice, Mr. Gruber," said Paddington, staring down at his plate with a puzzled expression on his face. "But I think I've lost one of my onions."

"You've what?" asked Mr. Brown. It was difficult to hear what Paddington was saying for the noise the orchestra was making. It had been playing quite sweetly up until a moment ago but suddenly it had started making a dreadful row. It was something to do with one of the saxophone players in the front row. He kept shaking his instrument and then trying to blow it, and all the while the conductor was glaring at him.

"My onion!" exclaimed Paddington. "I had six just now

and when I put my fork on one of them it suddenly disappeared. Now I've only got five."

Mrs. Brown began to look more and more embarrassed as Paddington got down off his seat and began peering under the tables. "I do hope he finds it soon," she said. Everyone in the restaurant seemed to be looking in their direction and if they weren't actually pointing she knew they were talking about them.

"Gosh!" exclaimed Jonathan suddenly. He pointed towards the orchestra. "There *is* Paddington's onion!"

The Browns turned and looked at the orchestra. The saxophone player seemed to be having an argument with the conductor.

"How can I be expected to play properly," he said bitterly, "when I've got an onion in my instrument? And I've a good idea where it came from too!"

The conductor followed his gaze towards the Browns, who hurriedly looked the other way.

"For heaven's sake don't tell Paddington," said Mrs. Brown. "He'll only want it back."

"Never mind," said Mr. Gruber, as the door leading to the kitchen opened. "I think my omelet's just coming."

The Browns watched as a waiter entered bearing a silver dish which he placed on a small spirit stove near their table. Mr. Gruber had ordered an omelet "flambée", which meant it was set on fire just before it was served. "I don't know when I had one of those last," he said. "I'm looking forward to it."

"I must say it looks very nice," said Mr. Brown, twirling his moustache thoughtfully. "I rather wish I'd ordered one myself now."

"Come along, Paddington," he called, as the waiter set light to the pan. "Come and see Mr. Gruber's omelet. It's on fire."

"What!" cried Paddington, poking his head out from beneath the table. "Mr. Gruber's omelet's on fire?"

He stared in astonishment at the waiter as he bore the silver tray with its flaming omelet towards the table.

"It's all right, Mr. Gruber," he called, waving his paws in the air. "I'm coming!"

Before the Browns could stop him, Paddington had grabbed his paw bowl and had thrown the contents over the tray. There was a loud hissing noise and before the astonished gaze of the waiter Mr. Gruber's omelet slowly collapsed into a soggy mess in the bottom of the dish.

Several people near the Browns applauded. "What an unusual idea," said one of them. "Having the cabaret act sit at one of the tables just like anyone else."

One old gentleman in particular who was sitting by himself at the next table laughed no end. He had been watching Paddington intently for some time and now he began slapping his knee at each new happening.

"Crikey!" said Jonathan. "We're for it now." He pointed towards a party of very important-looking people, led by the head waiter, who were approaching the Browns' table.

They stopped a few feet away and the head waiter pointed at Paddington. "That's the one," he said. "The one with the whiskers!"

The most important-looking man stepped forward. "I am the manager," he announced. "And I'm afraid I must' ask you to leave. Throwing water over a waiter. Putting onions in a saxophone. Ordering marmalade sandwiches. You'll get the Porchester a bad name."

Mr. and Mrs. Brown exchanged glances. "I've never heard of such a thing," said Mrs. Bird. "If that bear goes we all go."

"Hear! Hear!" echoed Mr. Gruber.

'And if you go I shall go too," came a loud voice from the next table.

Everyone looked round as the old gentleman who had

been watching the proceedings rose and waved a finger at the manager. "May I ask why this young bear's being asked to leave?" he boomed.

The manager began to look even more worried, for the old gentleman was one of his best customers and he didn't want to offend him. "It annoys the other diners," he said.

"Nonsense!" boomed the old gentleman. "I'm one of the other diners and I'm not annoyed. Best thing that's happened in years. Don't know when I've enjoyed myself so much." He looked down at Paddington. "I should like to shake you by the paw, bear. It's about time this place was livened up a bit."

"Thank you very much," said Paddington, holding out his paw. He was a bit overawed by the old gentleman and he wasn't at all sure what it was all about anyway.

The old gentleman waved the waiters and the manager to one side and then turned to Mr. Brown. "I'd better introduce myself," he said. "I am Sir Huntley Martin the marmalade king."

"I've been in marmalade for fifty years," he boomed, "and been comin' here for thirty. Never heard anyone ask for a marmalade sandwich before. Does me old heart good."

Paddington looked most impressed. "Fancy being in marmalade for fifty years!" he exclaimed.

"I hope you'll allow me to join you," said Sir Huntley. "I've done a good many things in my life but I don't think I've ever been to a bear's birthday party before."

The old gentleman's presence seemed to have a magical

effect on the manager of the Porchester, for he had a hurried conference with the head waiter and in no time at all a procession started from the kitchen headed by a waiter bearing a silver tray on which was another omelet for Mr. Gruber.

Even the head waiter allowed himself a smile and he gave Paddington a special autographed menu to take away as a souvenir and promised that in future there would always be a special section for marmalade sandwiches.

It was a hilarious party of Browns who finally got up to go. Paddington was so full of good things he had a job to get up at all. He had a last lingering look at the remains of an ice-cream on his plate but decided that enough was as good as a feast. He'd enjoyed himself no end and after a great deal of thought he left a penny under his plate for the waiter.

Sir Huntley Martin seemed very sad that it had all come to an end. "Most enjoyable," he kept booming as they left the table. "Most enjoyable. Perhaps," he added hopefully to Paddington, "you'll do me the honour of visiting my factory one of these days."

"Oh, yes, please," said Paddington. "I should like that very much."

As they left the restaurant he waved good-bye with his paw to all the other diners, several of whom applauded when the orchestra struck up "Happy Birthday to You."

Only Mrs. Bird seemed less surprised than the others, for she had seen Sir Huntley slip something in the conductor's hand.

It had become really dark outside while they had been eating their dinner and all the lights in the street were on. After they had said good-bye to Sir Huntley, and because it was a special occasion, Mr. Brown drove round Piccadilly Circus so that Paddington could see all the coloured signs working.

Paddington peered out of the car window and his eyes grew larger and larger at the sight of all the red, green and blue lights flashing on and off and making patterns in the sky.

"Have you enjoyed yourself, Paddington?" asked Mr. Brown as they went round for the second time.

"Yes, thank you very much, Mr. Brown," exclaimed Paddington.

Altogether Paddington thought it had been a wonderful day and he was looking forward to writing a letter to his Aunt Lucy telling her everything about it.

After giving a final wave of his paw to some passers-by, he raised his hat to a policeman who signalled them on, and then settled back in his seat to enjoy the journey home with Mr. Gruber and the Browns.

"I think," he announced sleepily, as he gave one final stare at the fast-disappearing lights, "I would like to have an anniversary every year!"

"And so say all of us, Mr. Brown," echoed Mr. Gruber from the back of the car. "And so say all of us!"

CHAPTER FOUR

A Visit to the Bank

"Paddington looks unusually smart this morning," said Mrs. Bird.

"Oh, dear," said Mrs. Brown. "Does he? I hope he's not up to anything."

She joined Mrs. Bird at the window and followed the direction of her gaze up the road to where a small figure in a blue duffle coat was hurrying along the pavement.

Now that Mrs. Bird mentioned it Paddington did seem to have an air about him. Even from a distance his fur looked remarkably neat and freshly combed, and his old hat, instead of being pulled down over his ears, was set at a very rakish angle with the brim turned up, which was most unusual. Even his old suitcase looked as if it had had some kind of polish on it.

"He's not even going in his usual direction," said Mrs. Brown as Paddington, having reached the end of the road, looked carefully over his shoulder and then turned right and disappeared from view. "He *always* turns left."

"If you ask me," said Mrs. Bird, "that young bear's got something on his mind. He was acting strangely at breakfast this morning. He didn't even have a second helping and he kept peering over Mr. Brown's shoulder at the paper with a very odd look on his face."

"I'm not surprised he had an odd look if it was Henry's paper," said Mrs. Brown. "I can never make head or tail of it myself."

Mr. Brown worked in the City of London and he always read a very important newspaper at breakfast time, full of news about stocks and shares and other money matters, which the rest of the Browns found very dull.

"All the same," she continued, as she led the way into the kitchen, "it's very strange. I do hope he hasn't got one of his ideas coming on. He spent most of yesterday evening doing his accounts and that's often a bad sign."

Mrs. Brown and Mrs. Bird were hard at work preparing for the coming holiday, and with only a few days left there were a thousand and one things to be done. If they hadn't been quite so busy they might well have put two and two together, but as it was the matter of Paddington's strange behaviour was soon forgotten in the rush to get everything ready.

Unaware of the interest he had caused, Paddington made his way along a road not far from the Portobello market until he reached an imposing building which stood slightly apart from the rest. It had tall, bronze doors which were tightly shut, and over the entrance, in large gold letters, were the words FLOYDS BANK LIMITED.

After carefully making sure that no one was watching, Paddington withdrew a small cardboard-covered book from under his hat and then sat down on his suitcase outside the bank while he waited for the doors to open.

Like the building, the book had the words FLOYDS BANK printed on the outside, and just inside the front cover it had P. BROWN ESQ., written in ink.

With the exception of the Browns and Mr. Gruber not many people knew about Paddington's banking account as it was a closely kept secret. It had all started some months before when Paddington came across an advertisement in one of Mr. Brown's old newspapers which he cut out and saved. In it a very fatherly-looking man smoking a pipe, who said he was a Mr. Floyd, explained how any money left with him would earn what he called "interest", and that the longer he kept it the more it would be worth.

Paddington had an eye for a bargain and having his money increase simply by leaving it somewhere had sounded like a very good bargain indeed.

The Browns had been so pleased at the idea that Mr. Brown had given him three shillings to add to his Christmas and birthday money, and after a great deal of thought Paddington had himself added another sixpence which he'd carefully saved from his weekly bun allowance. When all these sums were added together they made a grand total of one pound, three shillings and sixpence, and one day Mrs. Bird had taken him along to the bank in order to open an account.

For several days afterwards Paddington had hung about in a shop doorway opposite casting suspicious glances at anyone who went in or out. But after having been moved on by a passing policeman he'd had to let matters rest.

Since then, although he had carefully checked the amount in his book several times, Paddington had never actually been inside the bank. Secretly he was rather overawed by all the marble and thick polished wood, so he was pleased when at long last ten o'clock began to strike on a nearby church clock and he was still the only one outside.

As the last of the chimes died away there came the sound of bolts being withdrawn on the other side of the door, and Paddington hurried forward to peer eagerly through the letter-box.

"'Ere, 'ere," exclaimed the porter, as he caught sight of Paddington's hat through the slit. "No hawkers 'ere, young feller-me-lad. This is a bank — not a workhouse. We don't want no hobbledehoys hanging around here."

"Hobbledehoys?" repeated Paddington, letting go of the letter-box flap in his surprise.

"That's what I said," grumbled the porter as he opened the door. "Breathing all over me knockers. I 'as to polish that brass, yer know."

"I'm not a hobbledehoy," exclaimed Paddington,

looking most offended as he waved his bank book in the air. "I'm a bear and I've come to see Mr. Floyd about my savings."

"Ho, dear," said the porter, taking a closer look at Paddington. "Beggin' yer pardon, sir. When I saw your whiskers poking through me letter-box I mistook you for one of them bearded gentlemen of the road."

"That's all right," said Paddington sadly. "I often get mistaken." And as the man held the door open for him he raised his hat politely and hurried into the bank.

On several occasions in the past Mrs. Bird had impressed on Paddington how wise it was to have money in the bank in case of a rainy day and how he might be glad of it one day for a special occasion. Thinking things over in bed the night before, Paddington had decided that going abroad for a holiday was very much a special occasion, and after studying the advertisement once again he had thought up a very good idea for having the best of both worlds, but like many ideas he had at night under the bedclothes it didn't seem quite such a good one in the cold light of day.

Now that he was actually inside the bank, Paddington began to feel rather guilty and he wished he'd consulted Mr. Gruber on the matter, for he wasn't at all sure that Mrs. Bird would approve of his taking any money out without first asking her.

Hurrying across to one of the cubby-holes in the counter, Paddington climbed up on his suitcase and peered over the edge. The man on the other side looked rather startled when Paddington's hat appeared over the top and he reached nervously for a nearby ink-well.

"I'd like to take out all my savings for a special occasion, please," said Paddington importantly, as he handed the man his book.

Looking rather relieved, the man took Paddington's book from him and then raised one eyebrow as he held it up to the light. There were a number of calculations in red ink all over the cover, not to mention blots and one or two rather messy-looking marmalade stains.

"I'm afraid I had an accident with one of my jars under the bedclothes last night," explained Paddington hastily as he caught the man's eye.

"One of your *jars?*" repeated the man. "Under the *bedclothes?*"

"That's right," said Paddington. "I was working out my interest and I stepped back into it by mistake. It's a bit difficult under the bedclothes."

"It must be," said the man distastefully. "Marmalade stains indeed! And on a Floyds bank book!"

He hadn't been with the branch for very long, and although the manager had told him they sometimes had some very odd customers to deal with, nothing had been mentioned about bears' banking accounts.

"What would you like me to do with it?" he asked doubtfully.

"I'd like to leave all my interest in, please," explained Paddington. "In case it rains."

"Well," said the man in a superior tone of voice as he

made some calculations on a piece of paper. "I'm afraid you won't keep very dry on this. It only comes to threepence."

"*What!*" exclaimed Paddington, hardly able to believe his ears. "*Threepence!* I don't think that's very interesting."

"Interest isn't the same thing as interesting," said the man. "Not the same thing at all."

He tried hard to think of some way of explaining matters for he wasn't used to dealing with bears and he had a feeling that Paddington was going to be one of his more difficult customers.

"It's...it's something we give you for letting us borrow

your money," he said. "The longer you leave it in the more you get."

"Well, my money's been in since just after Christmas," explained Paddington. "That's nearly six months."

"Threepence," said the man firmly.

Paddington watched in a daze as the man made an entry in his book and then pushed a one-pound note and some silver across the counter. "There you are," he said briskly. "One pound, three shillings and sixpence."

Paddington looked suspiciously at the note and then consulted a piece of paper he held in his paw. His eyes grew larger and larger as he compared the two.

"I think you must have made a mistake," he exclaimed. "This isn't my note."

"A mistake?" said the man stiffly. "We of Floyds never make mistakes."

"But it's got a different number," said Paddington hotly.

"A *different number*?" repeated the man.

"Yes," said Paddington. "And it said on mine that you promised to pay bear one pound on demand."

"Not *bear,*" said the assistant. "Bear*er*. It says that on all notes. Besides," he continued, "you don't get the same note back that you put in. I expect yours is miles away by now if it's anywhere at all. It might even have been burnt if it was an old one. They often burn old notes when they're worn out."

"*Burnt?*" repeated Paddington in a dazed voice. "*You've burnt my note?*"

"I didn't say it *had* been," said the man, looking more and more confused. "I only said it might have been."

Paddington took a deep breath and gave the assistant a hard stare. It was one of the extra special hard ones which his Aunt Lucy had taught him and which he kept for emergencies.

"I think I should like to see Mr. Floyd," he exclaimed.

"Mr. Floyd?" repeated the assistant. He mopped his brow nervously as he looked anxiously over Paddington's shoulder at the queue which was already beginning to form. There were some nasty murmurings going on at the back which he didn't like the sound of at all. "I'm afraid there isn't a Mr. Floyd," he said.

"We have a Mr. Trimble," he added hastily, as Paddington gave him an even harder stare. "He's the manager. I think perhaps I'd better fetch him — he'll know what to do."

Paddington stared indignantly after the retreating figure of the clerk as he made his way towards a door marked MANAGER. The more he saw of things the less he liked the look of them. Not only did his note have a different number but he had just caught sight of the dates on the coins and they were quite different to those on the ones he had left. Apart from that his own coins had been highly polished, whereas these were old and very dull.

Paddington climbed down off his suitcase and pushed his way through the crowd with a determined expression on his face. Although he was only small, Paddington was a bear with a strong sense of right and wrong, especially when it came to money matters, and he felt it was high time he took matters into his own paws.

After he had made his way out of the bank Paddington hurried down the road in the direction of a red kiosk. Locked away in the secret compartment of his suitcase there was a note with some special instructions Mrs. Bird had written out for him in case of an emergency, together with four pennies. Thinking things over as he went along, Paddington decided it was very much a matter of an emergency, in fact he had a job to remember when he'd had a bigger one, and he was glad when at long last the telephone kiosk came into view and he saw it was empty.

"I don't know what's going on at the bank this morning," said Mrs. Brown as she closed the front door. "There was an enormous crowd outside when I came past."

"Perhaps there's been a robbery," said Mrs. Bird. "You read of such nasty goings on these days."

"I don't think it was a robbery," said Mrs. Brown vaguely. "It was more like an emergency of some kind. The police were there and an ambulance *and* the fire-brigade."

"H'mm!" said Mrs. Bird. "Well, I hope for all our sakes it isn't anything serious. Paddington's got all his money there and if there has been a raid we shall never hear the last of it."

Mrs. Bird paused as she was speaking and a thoughtful expression came over her face. "Talking of Paddington, have you seen him since he went out?" she asked.

61

"No," said Mrs. Brown. "Good heavens!" she exclaimed. "You don't think..."

"I'll get my hat," said Mrs. Bird. "And if Paddington's not somewhere at the bottom of it all I'll eat it on the way home!"

It took Mrs. Brown and Mrs. Bird some while to force their way through the crowd into the bank, and when they at last got inside their worst suspicions were realised, for there, sitting on his suitcase in the middle of a large crowd of officials, was the small figure of Paddington.

"What on earth's going on?" cried Mrs. Brown, as they pushed their way through to the front.

Paddington looked very thankful to see the others. Things had been going from bad to worse since he'd got back to the bank.

"I think my numbers have got mixed up by mistake, Mrs. Brown," he explained.

"Trying to do a young bear out of his life's savings, that's what's going on," cried someone at the back.

"Set fire to his notes, they did," cried someone else.

"'Undreds of pounds gone up in smoke, so they say," called out a street trader who knew Paddington by sight and had come into the bank to see what all the fuss was about.

"Oh, dear," said Mrs. Brown nervously. "I'm sure there must be some mistake. I don't think Floyds would ever do a thing like that on purpose."

"Indeed not, madam," exclaimed the manager as he stepped forward.

"My name's Trimble," he continued. "Can you vouch for this young bear?"

"Vouch for him?" said Mrs. Bird. "Why, I brought him here myself in the first place. He's a most respectable member of the family and very law-abiding."

"Respectable he may be," said a large policeman, as he licked his pencil, "but I don't know so much about being

63

law-abiding. Dialling 999 he was without proper cause. Calling out the police, not to mention the fire-brigade and an ambulance. It'll all have to be gone into in the proper manner."

Everyone stopped talking and looked down at Paddington.

"I was only trying to ring Mrs. Bird," said Paddington.

"Trying to ring Mrs. Bird?" repeated the policeman slowly, as he wrote it down in his notebook.

"That's right," explained Paddington. "I'm afraid I got my paw stuck in number nine, and every time I tried to get it out someone asked me what I wanted so I shouted for help."

Mr. Trimble coughed. "I think perhaps we had better go into my office," he said. "It all sounds most complicated and it's much quieter in there."

With that everyone agreed wholeheartedly. And Paddington, as he picked up his suitcase and followed the others into the manager's office, agreed most of all. Having a banking account was quite the most complicated thing he had ever come across.

It was some while before Paddington finally got through his explanations, but when he had finished everyone looked most relieved that the matter wasn't more serious. Even the policeman seemed quite pleased.

"It's a pity there aren't more public-spirited bears about," he said, shaking Paddington by the paw. "If everyone called for help when they saw anything suspicious we'd have a lot less work to do in the long run."

After everyone else had left, Mr. Trimble took Mrs. Brown, Mrs. Bird and Paddington on a tour of the strong-room to show them where all the money was kept, and he even gave Paddington a book of instructions so that he would know exactly what to do the next time he paid the bank a visit.

"I do hope you *won't* close your account, Mr. Brown," he said. "We of Floyds never like to feel we're losing a valued customer. If you like to leave your three and sixpence with us for safe keeping I'll let you have a brand-new one-pound note to take away for your holidays."

Paddington thanked Mr. Trimble very much for all his trouble and then considered the matter. "If you don't mind," he said at last, "I think I'd like a used one instead."

Paddington wasn't the sort of bear who believed in taking any chances, and although the crisp new note in the manager's hand looked very tempting he decided he would much prefer to have one that had been properly tested.

CHAPTER FIVE

A Day by the Sea

Mr. Brown stood at the open front door of number thirty-two Windsor Gardens and surveyed the morning sun peeping over the top of the houses opposite.

"Hands up all those in favour of a trip to the sea," he called, looking back over his shoulder.

"People who ask questions like that must expect trouble," said Mrs. Brown, after the hubbub had died down and the last of three pairs of feet disappeared hastily up the stairs as their owners went to pack.

"I notice you and Mrs. Bird didn't put up your hands, Mary," said Mr. Brown, looking rather hurt. "I can't think why."

"I've been on your trips before, Henry," replied Mrs. Brown ominously. "It usually takes me a week to get over them."

"And some of us have all the sandwiches to cut," said Mrs. Bird pointedly.

"Sandwiches?" echoed Mr. Brown. "Who said anything about taking sandwiches?" He waved his hand grandly in the air. "We'll have lunch in a restaurant. Hang the expense. It's a long time since we had a day out."

"Well," said Mrs. Brown doubtfully. "Don't say I didn't warn you."

Anything else she might have been about to say was lost as another clatter of pounding feet heralded the arrival back downstairs of Jonathan, Judy and Paddington together with all their belongings. Paddington in particular seemed to be very well laden. Apart from his suitcase and hat, which he was wearing as usual, he was also carrying his special seaside straw hat, a beach ball, a rubber bathing ring and a bucket and spade, together with a windmill on the end of a stick, a pair of binoculars and an assortment of maps.

Mrs. Brown gazed at the collection. "I'm sure they didn't have all this trouble on the Everest expedition," she exclaimed.

"I don't suppose they took any bears with them," replied Mrs. Bird. "That's why. And I'm quite sure they didn't leave a trail of last year's sand on their stairs before they left."

Paddington looked most upset as he peered out from

behind his bucket and listened to the remarks. He was a great believer in being prepared for any kind of emergency and from what he could remember of previous trips to the seaside all sorts of things could happen and usually did.

"Come along everyone," called Mr. Brown, hurriedly coming to his rescue. "If we don't make an early start we shall get caught up in the rush and then we shall never get there. A day at the sea will do us all good. It'll help blow some of the cobwebs out of your whiskers, Paddington."

Paddington pricked up his ears. "Blow some of the cobwebs out of my whiskers, Mr. Brown?" he exclaimed, looking even more upset as he followed the others out to the waiting car.

While Jonathan, Judy and Mr. Brown packed the equipment into the boot, and Mrs. Brown and Mrs. Bird went upstairs to change, Paddington stood on the front seat of the car and peered anxiously at his face in the driving mirror. There were several pieces of cotton stuck to his whiskers, not to mention some old marmalade and cocoa stains, but he couldn't see any signs of a spider let alone a cobweb.

Paddington was unusually silent on the journey down and he was still pondering over the matter later that morning when they swept over the brow of a hill and began the long descent towards Brightsea. But as they drew near the front the smell of the sea air and the sight of all the holidaymakers strolling along the promenade soon drove all other thoughts from his mind.

Paddington was very keen on outings, especially Mr.

Brown's unexpected seaside ones, and he stuck his head out of the front window of the car and peered round excitedly as they drove along the front looking for somewhere to park.

"All hands on deck," said Mr. Brown, as he backed the car into a vacant space. "Stand by to unload."

Paddington gathered his belongings and jumped out on to the pavement. "I'll find a place on the beach, Mr. Brown," he called eagerly.

In the back of the car Mrs. Brown and Mrs. Bird exchanged glances.

"I know one thing," said Mrs. Brown, as she helped Mrs. Bird out of the car. "They might not have had any bears with them on the Everest expedition but at least they had some Sherpas to help with their luggage. Just look at it all!"

"It won't take a minute, Mary," puffed Mr. Brown from behind a pile of carrier bags. "Where's Paddington? He said he'd find a spot for us."

"There he is," said Jonathan, pointing to a patch of sand where six deck chairs were already ranged in a row. "He's talking to that man with the ticket machine."

"Oh, dear," said Mrs. Brown anxiously. "He looks rather upset. I hope there's nothing wrong."

"Trust Paddington to get into trouble," said Judy. "We haven't been here a minute."

The Browns hurried down some steps leading to the beach and as they did so a familiar voice reached their ears.

"Three shillings!" exclaimed the voice bitterly. "Three

shillings just to sit in a deck chair!"

"No, mate," came the voice of the ticket man in reply.
"It's not three shillings just to sit in a deck chair. You've
got six chairs 'ere and they're sixpence each. Six sixes is
thirty-six."

Paddington looked more and more upset as he listened
to the man's words. He'd felt very pleased with himself
when he'd found the pile of chairs beside a patch of clean
sand but almost before he'd had time to arrange them in a
row, and certainly before he'd had a chance to test even one
of them, the man had appeared as if by magic from behind
a beach hut, waving his ticket machine as he pounced on
him.

"Three shillings!" he repeated, collapsing into the
nearest chair.

"I know your sort," lectured the man in a loud voice as
he looked around and addressed the rest of the beach.
"You sit down in them chairs and pretend you're asleep
when I comes round for the money. Or else you say yer
tickets 'ave blowed away. Your sort cost the Corporation
'undreds of pounds a year."

The man's voice trailed away as a muffled cry came from
somewhere near his feet.

"'Ere," he exclaimed, as he bent down and stared at a
heaving mass of striped canvas. "What's 'appened?"

"Help!" came the muffled voice again.

"Dear, oh dear," said the man as he disentangled
Paddington from the chair. "You couldn't have 'ad yer
back strut properly adjusted."

"My back strut!" exclaimed Paddington, sitting up.

"That's right," said the man. "You're supposed to fit it into the slots — not just rest it on the side. No wonder it collapsed."

Paddington gave the man a hard stare as he scrambled to his feet and undid his suitcase. Sixpence seemed a lot to pay just to sit in a chair at the best of times, but when it didn't even have any instructions and collapsed into the bargain, words failed him.

"Instructions?" echoed the man, as he took Paddington's money and rang up six tickets. "I've never 'eard of a deck chair 'aving instructions afore. You wants a lot for yer money."

"I hope you haven't been having any trouble," said Mr. Brown, as he hurried on to the scene and pressed something round and shiny into the man's hand.

"Trouble?" said the ticket man, his expression changing as he felt the coin. "Bless you no, sir. Just a slight misunderstanding as yer might say. Tell you what, guv," he continued, turning to Paddington and touching his cap with a more respectful air. "I know these days out at the seaside can come pretty expensive for a young bear gent what's standing treat. If you wants to get yer money back and make a profit into the bargain your best plan is to keep a weather eye open for Basil Budd."

"Basil Budd?" repeated Paddington, looking most surprised.

"That's right," said the man, pointing towards a large notice pasted on the sea wall. "He's in Brightsea today. It's one of them newspaper stunts. The first one as confronts 'im and says 'You're Basil Budd' gets five pounds reward. Only mind you're carrying one of 'is newspapers," he warned. "Otherwise 'e won't pay up."

So saying, he touched his cap once more and hurried off up the beach in the direction of some new arrivals, leaving the Browns to arrange themselves and their belongings on Paddington's patch of sand.

Mr. Brown turned to thank Paddington for standing treat with the deck chairs but already he had disappeared up the sand and was standing gazing at the poster on the sea wall with a thoughtful expression on his face.

The poster had the one word SENSATION written in large, red capital letters across the top. Underneath was a picture of a man in a trilby hat followed by the announcement that Basil Budd of the *Daily Globe* was in town.

The smaller print which followed went on to explain all that the deck-chair man had told them. It took Paddington some while to read all the poster, particularly as he read

72

some of the more interesting bits several times in case he'd made a mistake. But whichever way he read the notice it seemed that not only was Basil Budd anxious to give away five pound notes to anyone who confronted him, but that his own seaside outing would be ruined if he had so much as one note left at the end of the day.

"Good Heavens!" said Mr. Brown, as he glanced up the beach again. "Paddington *is* lashing out today. He's bought himself a newspaper now!"

"I pity the person who happens to look anything like Basil Budd," said Mrs. Bird. "I can see there'll be some nasty scenes if they don't pay up."

Mr. Brown wriggled into his costume. "Come on, Paddington," he called. "It's time for a bathe."

After taking one last look at the poster Paddington turned and came slowly back down the beach. Although he'd been looking forward all the morning to a paddle he was beginning to have second thoughts on the matter. Paddington liked dipping his paws in the sea as much as anyone but he didn't want to run the risk of missing five pounds reward if Basil Budd happened to stroll by while his back was turned.

"Perhaps he's having a paddle himself," said Mrs. Bird helpfully.

Paddington brightened at the thought. He took out his opera glasses and peered through them at the figures already in the water. There didn't seem to be any sign of a man wearing a trilby hat, but all the same a moment later he climbed into his rubber bathing ring and hurried down to the water's edge clutching the copy of the *Daily Globe* in one paw and his suitcase in the other.

Mrs. Bird sighed. Paddington was just too far away for her to make out the expression on his face, but she didn't at all like the look of the little she could see. From where she was sitting some of the stares he was giving passers-by seemed very hard ones indeed.

"Why can't we have a nice quiet day at the sea like any normal family?" she said.

"At least it keeps him out of mischief," replied Mrs. Brown. "And we know where he is which is something."

"That's not going to last very long," said Mrs. Bird, ominously, as she watched Paddington splash his way along the shore in the direction of the pier. "There's plenty of time yet. You mark my words."

Unaware of the anxious moments he was causing, Paddington plodded on his way, pausing every now and then to compare the picture on the front page of his paper with that of a passer-by.

The beach was beginning to fill up. There were fat men in shorts, thin men in bathing costumes, men of all shapes and sizes; some wore sun hats, some caps, others coloured hats made of cardboard, and once he even saw a man wearing a bowler, but as far as he could make out there wasn't one person along the whole of the Brightsea front who bore any resemblance to Basil Budd.

After making his way along the beach for the third time Paddington stopped by the pier and mopped his brow while he took another long look at a *Daily Globe* poster.

It was a strange thing but somehow with each journey up and down the beach the expression on Basil Budd's face seemed to change. At first it had been quite an ordinary, pleasant sort of face, but now that he looked at it more closely Paddington decided there was a mocking air about it which he didn't like the look of at all.

With a sigh he found himself a quiet corner of the beach and sat down with his back against a pile of deck chairs in order to consider the matter. Taken all round he was beginning to feel very upset at the way things were going. In fact, if he could have found the man who had sold him the newspaper he would have asked for his money back. But with every minute more and more people were streaming into Brightsea and the chances of finding the newspaper seller, let alone Basil Budd himself, seemed more and more remote.

As he sat there deep in thought Paddington's eyelids began to feel heavier and heavier. Several times he pushed them open with a paw but gradually the combination of a large breakfast, several ice-creams, and all the walks up and down the sand in the hot sun, not to mention the distant sound of waves breaking on the sea shore, grew too much for him, and a short while later some gentle snores added themselves to the general hubbub all around.

Mrs. Brown heaved a sigh of relief. "Thank goodness!" she exclaimed, as a small brown figure came hurrying along the promenade towards them. "I was beginning to think something had happened to him."

Mr. Brown removed his belongings from the only remaining chair at their table. "About time too," he grumbled. "I'm starving."

In order to avoid the crowds the Browns had arranged to meet for an early lunch on the terrace of a large Brightsea promenade hotel, and all the family with the exception of Paddington had arrived there in good time. Paddington had a habit of disappearing on occasions, but very rarely at meal times, and as the minutes ticked by and the other tables started to fill up the Browns had become more and more worried.

"Where on earth have you been?" asked Mrs. Brown, as Paddington drew near.

Paddington raised his hat with a distant expression on

his face. "I was having a bit of a dream, Mrs. Brown," he replied vaguely.

"A dream?" echoed Mrs. Bird. "I should have thought you had plenty of time for those at home."

"This was a special seaside one, Mrs. Bird," explained Paddington, looking slightly offended. "It was very unusual."

"It must have been," said Judy, "if it made you late for lunch."

Mr. Brown handed Paddington a large menu. "We've ordered you some soup to be going on with," he said. "Perhaps you'd like to choose what you want to follow..."

The Browns looked across at Paddington with some concern. He seemed to be acting most strangely. One moment he'd been about to sit down quietly in his chair, the next moment he had jumped up again and was peering through his opera glasses with an air of great excitement.

"Is anything the matter?" asked Mr. Brown.

Paddington adjusted his glasses. "I think that's Basil Budd," he exclaimed, pointing towards a man at the next table.

"Basil Budd?" echoed Mrs. Brown. 'But it can't be. He's got a beard."

"Basil Budd hasn't," said Jonathan. "I've seen his picture on the posters."

Paddington looked even more mysterious. "That's what my dream was about," he said. "Only I don't think it was a dream after all. I'm going to confront him!"

"Oh, dear," said Mrs. Brown nervously, as Paddington

stood up. "Do you think you should?"

But her words fell on deaf ears for Paddington was already tapping the bearded man on his shoulder. "I'd like my five pounds, please, Mr. Budd," he announced, holding up his copy of the *Daily Globe*.

The man paused with a soup spoon halfway to his mouth. "No, thank you," he said, looking at the newspaper. "I've got one already."

"I'm not a newspaper bear," said Paddington patiently. "I think you're Basil Budd of the *Daily Globe* and I've come to confront you."

"You've come to confront me?" repeated the man, as if in a dream. "But my name isn't Budd. I've never even heard of him."

Paddington took a deep breath and gave the man the hardest stare he could manage. "If you don't give me my five pounds," he exclaimed hotly. "I shall call a policeman!"

The man returned Paddington's stare with one almost as hard. "*You'll* call a policeman!" he exclaimed. "If you don't go away, bear, that's just what I intend doing."

Paddington was a bear with a strong sense of right and wrong and for a moment he stood rooted to the spot looking as if he could hardly believe his eyes, let alone his ears. Then suddenly, before the astonished gaze of the Browns and everyone else on the hotel terrace, he reached forward and gave the man's beard a determined tug with both paws.

If the other occupants of the hotel were taken aback by

the unexpected turn of events the man with the beard was even more upset, and a howl of anguish rang round the terrace as he jumped up clutching his chin.

Paddington's jaw dropped open and a look of alarm came over his face as he examined his empty paws. "Excuse me," he exclaimed, raising his hat politely. "I think I must have made a mistake."

"A mistake!" spluttered the man, dabbing at his lap with a napkin where a large soup stain had appeared. "Where's the manager! I want to see the manager. I demand an explanation."

"I've got an explanation," said Paddington unhappily, "but I'm not sure if it's a good one."

"Oh, crikey," groaned Jonathan, as a man in a black suit came hurrying on to the scene closely followed by several waiters. "Here we go again!"

"I've never," said Mrs. Bird, "met such a bear for getting into hot water. Now what are we going to do?"

Mr. Brown sat back in the Brightsea hotel manager's office and stared at Paddington. "Do you mean to say," he exclaimed, "you actually saw a man putting on a false beard behind a pile of deck chairs?"

"There were two of them," said Paddington importantly. "I thought I was having a dream and then they went away and I found I was really awake all the time."

"But I still don't see why you thought it was the man from the *Daily Globe*," said Mrs. Brown.

"I'm afraid this young bear got his 'buds' mixed," said a policeman. "Quite a natural mistake in the circumstances."

"You see, he'd stumbled on South Coast Charlie and his pal," said a second policeman. "They always call each other 'bud'. I think they've been seeing too many films on television."

"South Coast Charlie!" echoed Mrs. Bird. "Goodness me!"

"They tour all the south coast holiday resorts during the summer months doing confidence tricks," continued the first policeman. "We've been after them for some time now but they've always kept one step ahead of us. Kept changing their disguises. Thanks to this young bear's description we've a good idea who to look for now. In fact, I daresay there'll be some kind of a reward."

The Browns looked at one another. After the excitement earlier on, the hotel manager's office seemed remarkably peaceful. Even the man with the beard, now that he had got over his first surprise, looked most impressed by Paddington's explanation. "I've been mistaken for a few people in my time," he said, "but never a Basil Budd let alone a South Coast Charlie."

"Trust Paddington to find someone with a beard sitting at the next table," said Jonathan.

The hotel manager coughed. "That's not really so surprising," he said. "There's a magicians' conference on at Brightsea this week and a lot of them are staying at this hotel. You'll see a good many beards."

"Good gracious!" said Mrs. Bird, as she looked through the office window. "You're quite right. Look at them all!"

The others followed the direction of Mrs. Bird's gaze. Now that it had been mentioned there were beards everywhere. Long beards, short ones, whiskery beards and neatly trimmed ones. "I don't think I've ever seen so many before," said Mr. Brown. "I suppose that's why South Coast Charlie wore one?"

"That's right, sir," said one of the policemen. "It's a good thing this young gentleman didn't try them all. We might have had a nasty scene on our hands."

"Perhaps you'd care to join me for lunch," said the man with the beard, addressing the Browns as the policemen stood up to go. "I'm a magician myself," he continued, turning to Paddington. "The Great Umberto. I might even be able to show you a few tricks while we eat."

"Thank you very much, Mr. Umberto," said Paddington, as the hotel manager hurried on ahead to reserve a table. "I should like that."

Altogether Paddington was beginning to think it was a very good day out at the sea after all. Although he hadn't managed to win five pounds by confronting Basil Budd he was very keen on tricks and the prospect of having lunch with a real magician sounded most exciting.

"Hmm," said Mrs. Bird, as she followed the others out on to the hotel terrace. "We may be having lunch with a magician but I have a feeling that even the Great Umberto won't be able to make his meal disappear as quickly as Paddington."

Paddington pricked up his ears in agreement as he caught Mrs. Bird's remark. It was already long past his lunch time and detective work, especially seaside detective work, used up a lot of energy.

"I don't think I shall have many cobwebs left in my whiskers after today, Mr. Brown," he announced amid general agreement, as he sat down at the table to enjoy a well-earned lunch.

CHAPTER SIX

Something Nasty in the Kitchen

"Two days!" exclaimed Mrs. Brown, staring at Doctor MacAndrew in horror. "Do you mean to say we've to stay in bed for two whole days?"

"Aye," said Doctor MacAndrew. "There's a nasty wee bug going the rounds and if ye don't I'll no' be responsible for the consequences."

"But Mrs. Bird's away until tomorrow," said Mrs. Brown. "And so are Jonathan and Judy...and...and that only leaves Paddington."

"Two days," repeated Doctor MacAndrew as he snapped his bag shut. "And not a moment less. The house'll no' fall down in that time."

"There's one thing," he added, as he paused at the door and stared at Mr. and Mrs. Brown with a twinkle in his eye. "Whatever else happens you'll no die of starvation. Yon wee bear's verra fond of his inside!"

With that he went downstairs to tell Paddington the news.

"Oh, dear," groaned Mr. Brown, as the door closed behind the doctor. "I think I feel worse already."

Paddington felt most important as he listened to what Doctor MacAndrew had to say and he carefully wrote down all the instructions. After he had shown him to the door and waved good-bye he hurried back into the kitchen to collect his shopping basket on wheels.

Usually with Paddington shopping in the market was a very leisurely affair. He liked to stop and have a chat with the various traders in the Portobello Road, where he was a well-known figure. To have Paddington's custom was considered to be something of an honour as he had a very good eye for a bargain. But on this particular morning he hardly had time even to call in at the bakers for his morning supply of buns.

It was early and Mr. Gruber hadn't yet opened his shutters, so Paddington wrapped one of the hot buns in a piece of paper, wrote a message on the outside saying who it was from and explaining that he wouldn't be along for "elevenses" that morning, and then pushed it through the letter-box.

Having finished the shopping and been to the chemist

with Doctor MacAndrew's prescription, Paddington made his way quickly back to number thirty-two Windsor Gardens.

It wasn't often Paddington had a chance to lend a paw around the house, let alone cook the dinner, and he was looking forward to it. In particular, there was a new feather duster of Mrs. Bird's he'd had his eye on for several days and which he was anxious to test.

"I must say Paddington looks very professional in that old apron of Mrs. Bird's," said Mrs. Brown later that morning. She sat up in bed holding a cup and saucer. "And it was kind of him to bring us up a cup of coffee."

"Very kind," agreed Mr. Brown. "But I rather wish he hadn't brought all these sandwiches as well."

"They *are* rather thick," agreed Mrs. Brown, looking at one doubtfully. "He said they were emergency ones. I'm not quite sure what he meant by that. I do hope nothing's wrong."

"I don't like the sound of it," said Mr. Brown. "There've been several nasty silences this morning — as if something were going on." He sniffed. "And there seems to be a strong smell of burnt feathers coming from somewhere."

"Well, you'd better eat them, Henry," warned Mrs. Brown. "He's used some of his special marmalade from the cut-price grocer and I'm sure they're meant to be a treat. You'll never hear the last of it if you leave any."

"Yes, but *six!*" grumbled Mr. Brown. "I'm not even very keen on marmalade. And at twelve o'clock in the

85

morning! I shan't want any lunch." He looked thoughtfully at the window and then at the plate of sandwiches again.

"No, Henry," said Mrs. Brown, reading his thoughts. "You're not giving any to the birds. I don't suppose they like marmalade."

"Anyway," she added, "Paddington did say something about lunch being late, so you may be glad of them."

She looked wistfully at the door. "All the same, I wish I could see what's going on. It's not knowing that's the worst part. He had flour all over his whiskers when he came up just now."

"If you ask me," said Mr. Brown, "you're probably much better off being in the dark." He took a long drink from his cup and then jumped up in bed, spluttering.

"Henry, dear," exclaimed Mrs. Brown. "*Do* be careful. You'll have coffee all over the sheets."

"Coffee!" yelled Mr. Brown. "Did you say this was coffee?"

"*I* didn't, dear," said Mrs. Brown mildly. "Paddington did." She took a sip from her own cup and then made a wry face. "It *has* got rather an unusual taste."

"Unusual!" exclaimed Mr. Brown. "It tastes like nothing on earth." He glared at his cup and then poked at it gingerly with a spoon. "It's got some funny green things floating in it too!" he exclaimed.

"Have a marmalade sandwich," said Mrs. Brown. "It'll help take the taste away."

Mr. Brown gave his wife an expressive look. "Two

days!" he said, sinking back into the bed. "Two whole days!"

Downstairs, Paddington was in a bit of a mess. So, for that matter was the kitchen, the hall, the dining-room and the stairs.

Things hadn't really gone right since he'd lifted up a corner of the dining-room carpet in order to sweep some dust underneath and had discovered a number of very interesting old newspapers. Paddington sighed. Perhaps if he hadn't spent so much time reading the newspapers he might not have hurried quite so much over the rest of the dusting. Then he might have been more careful when he shook Mrs. Bird's feather duster over the boiler.

And if he hadn't set fire to Mrs. Bird's feather duster he might have been able to take more time over the coffee.

Paddington felt very guilty about the coffee and he rather wished he had tested it before taking it upstairs to Mr. and Mrs. Brown. He was very glad he'd decided to make cocoa for himself instead.

Quite early in the morning Paddington had run out of saucepans. It was the first big meal he had ever cooked and he wanted it to be something special. Having carefully consulted Mrs. Bird's cookery book he'd drawn out a special menu in red ink with a bit of everything on it.

But by the time he had put the stew to boil in one big saucepan, the potatoes in another saucepan, the peas in a third, the brussels sprouts in yet another, and used at least four more for mixing operations, there was really only the electric kettle left in which to put the cabbage. Unfortunately, in his haste to make the coffee, Paddington had completely forgotten to take the cabbage out again.

Now he was having trouble with the dumplings!

Paddington was very keen on stew, especially when it was served with dumplings, but he was beginning to wish he had decided to cook something else for lunch.

Even now he wasn't quite sure what had gone wrong. He'd looked up the chapter on dumplings in Mrs. Bird's cookery book and followed the instructions most carefully; putting two parts of flour to one of suet and then adding milk before stirring the whole lot together. But somehow, instead of the mixture turning into neat balls as it showed in the coloured picture, it had all gone runny. Then, when he'd added more flour and suet, it had gone lumpy instead and stuck to his fur, so that he'd had to add more milk and then more flour and suet, until he had a huge mountain of dumpling mixture in the middle of the kitchen table.

All in all, he decided, it just wasn't his day. He wiped his paws carefully on Mrs. Bird's apron and, after looking around in vain for a large enough bowl, scraped the dumpling mixture into his hat.

It was a lot heavier than he had expected and he had a job lifting it up on to the stove. It was even more difficult putting the mixture into the stew as it kept sticking to his paws and as fast as he got it off one paw it stuck to the other. In the end he had to sit on the draining board and use the broom handle.

Paddington wasn't very impressed with Mrs. Bird's

cookery book. The instructions seemed all wrong. Not only had the dumplings been difficult to make, but the ones they showed in the picture were much too small. They weren't a bit like the ones Mrs. Bird usually served. Even Paddington rarely managed more than two of Mrs. Bird's dumplings.

Having scraped the last of the mixture off his paws Paddington pushed the saucepan lid hard down and scrambled clear. The steam from the saucepan had made his fur go soggy and he sat in the middle of the floor for several minutes getting his breath back and mopping his brow with an old dish-cloth.

It was while he was sitting there, scraping the remains of

89

the dumplings out of his hat and licking the spoon, that he felt something move behind him. Not only that, but out of the corner of his eye he could see a shadow on the floor which definitely hadn't been there a moment before.

Paddington sat very still, holding his breath and listening. It wasn't so much a noise as a feeling, and it seemed to be creeping nearer and nearer, making a soft swishing noise as it came. Paddington felt his fur begin to stand on end as there came the sound of a slow plop...plop...plop across the kitchen floor. And then, just as he was summoning up enough courage to look over his shoulder, there was a loud crash from the direction of the stove. Without waiting to see what it was Paddington pulled his hat down over his head and ran, slamming the door behind him.

He arrived in the hall just as there was a loud knock on the front door. To his relief he heard a familiar voice call his name through the letter-box.

"I got your message, Mr. Brown — about not being able to come for elevenses this morning," began Mr. Gruber, as Paddington opened the door, "and I just thought I would call round to see if there was anything I could do..." His voice trailed away as he stared at Paddington.

"Why, Mr. Brown," he exclaimed. "You're all white! Is anything the matter?"

"Don't worry, Mr. Gruber," cried Paddington, waving his paws in the air. "It's only some of Mrs. Bird's flour. I'm afraid I can't raise my hat because it's stuck down with dumpling mixture — but I'm very glad you've come because there's something nasty in the kitchen!"

"Something nasty in the kitchen?" echoed Mr. Gruber. "What sort of thing?"

"I don't know," said Paddington , struggling with his hat. "But it's got a shadow and it's making a funny noise."

Mr. Gruber looked around nervously for something to defend himself with. "We'll soon see about that," he said, taking a warming pan off the wall.

Paddington led the way back to the kitchen and then stood to one side by the door. "After you, Mr. Gruber," he said politely.

"Er...thank you, Mr. Brown," said Mr. Gruber doubtfully.

He grasped the warming pan firmly in both hands and then kicked open the door. "Come out!" he cried. "Whoever you are!"

"I don't think it's a *who*, Mr. Gruber," said Paddington, peering round the door. "It's a *what!*"

"Good heavens!" exclaimed Mr. Gruber, staring at the sight which met his eyes. "What *has* been going on?"

Over most of the kitchen there was a thin film of flour. There was flour on the table, in the sink, on the floor; in fact, over practically everything. But it wasn't the general state of the room which made Mr. Gruber cry out with surprise — it was the sight of something large and white hanging over the side of the stove.

He stared at it for a moment and then advanced cautiously across the kitchen and poked it with the handle of the warming pan. There was a loud squelching noise and Mr. Gruber jumped back as part of it broke away and fell with a plop to the floor.

"Good heavens!" he exclaimed again. "I do believe it's some kind of dumpling, Mr. Brown. I've never seen quite such a big one before," he went on as Paddington joined him. "It's grown right out of the saucepan and pushed the lid on the floor. No wonder it made you jump."

Mr. Gruber mopped his brow and opened the window. It was very warm in the kitchen. "How ever did it get to be that size?"

"I don't really know, Mr. Gruber," said Paddington

92

looking puzzled. "It's one of mine and it didn't start off that way. I think something must have gone wrong in the saucepan."

"I should think it has," said Mr. Gruber. "If I were you, Mr. Brown, I think I'd turn the cooker off before it catches fire and does any more damage. There's no knowing what might happen once it gets out of control.

"Perhaps, if you'll allow me," he continued tactfully, "I can give you a hand. It must be very difficult cooking for so many people."

"It is when you only have paws, Mr. Gruber," said Paddington gratefully.

Mr. Gruber sniffed. "I must say it all smells very nice. If we make some more dumplings quickly everything else should be just about ready."

As he handed Paddington the flour and suet Mr. Gruber explained how dumplings became very much larger when they were cooked and that it really needed only a small amount of mixture to make quite large ones.

"No wonder yours were so big, Mr. Brown," he said, as he lifted Paddington's old dumpling into the washing-up bowl. "You must have used almost a bag of flour."

"Two bags," said Paddington, looking over his shoulder. "I don't know what Mrs. Bird will say when she hears about it."

"Perhaps, if we buy her some more," said Mr. Gruber, as he staggered into the garden with the bowl, "she won't mind quite so much."

93

"That's queer," said Mr. Brown, as he stared out of the bedroom window. "There's a big white thing suddenly appeared in the garden. Just behind the nasturtiums."

"Nonsense, Henry," said Mrs. Brown. "You must be seeing things."

"I'm not," said Mr. Brown, rubbing his glasses and taking another look. "It's all white and shapeless and it looks horrible. Mr. Curry's seen it too — he's peering over the fence at it now. Do *you* know what it is, Paddington?"

"A big white thing, Mr. Brown?" repeated Paddington vaguely, joining him at the window. "Perhaps it's a snowball."

"In summer?" said Mr. Brown suspiciously.

"Henry," said Mrs. Brown. "Do come away from there and decide what you're having for lunch. Paddington's gone to a lot of trouble writing out a menu for us."

Mr. Brown took a large sheet of drawing paper from his wife and his face brightened as he studied it. It said:

MENUE

SOOP

FISH
OMMLETS
ROWST BEEF
STEW with Dumplings — POTATOES —
Brussle sprouts — Pees — Cabbidge Greyly

MARMALADE and Custerd

COFFEY

"How nice!" exclaimed Mr. Brown, when he had finished reading it. "And what a good idea putting pieces of vegetable on the side as illustrations. I've never seen that done before."

"They're not really meant to be there, Mr. Brown," said Paddington. "I'm afraid they came off my paws."

"Oh," said Mr. Brown, brushing his moustache thoughtfully. "Mmm. Well, you know, I rather fancy some soup and fish myself."

"I'm afraid they're off," said Paddington hastily, remembering a time when he'd once been taken out to lunch and they had arrived late.

"Off?" said Mr. Brown. "But they can't be. No one's ordered anything yet."

Mrs. Brown drew him to one side. "I think we're meant to have the stew and dumplings, Henry," she whispered. "They're underlined."

"What's that, Mary?" asked Mr. Brown, who was a bit slow to grasp things at times. "Oh! Oh, I see...er...on second thoughts, Paddington, I think perhaps I'll have the stew."

"That's good," said Paddington, "because I've got it on a tray outside all ready."

"By Jove," said Mr. Brown, as Paddington staggered in breathing heavily and carrying first one plate and then another piled high with stew. "I must say I didn't expect anything like this."

"Did you cook it all by yourself, Paddington?" asked Mrs. Brown.

"Well…almost all," replied Paddington truthfully. "I had a bit of an accident with the dumplings and so Mr. Gruber helped me make some more."

"You're sure you have enough for your own lunch?" said Mrs. Brown anxiously.

"Oh, yes," said Paddington, trying hard not to picture the kitchen, "there's enough to last for days and days."

"Well, I think you should be congratulated," said Mr. Brown. "I'm enjoying it no end. I bet there aren't many bears who can say they've cooked a meal like this. It's fit for a queen."

Paddington's eyes lit up with pleasure as he listened to Mr. and Mrs. Brown. It had been a lot hard of work but he was glad it had all been worth while — even if there was a lot of mess to clear up.

"You know, Henry," said Mrs. Brown, as Paddington hurried off downstairs to see Mr. Gruber, "we ought to think ourselves very lucky having a bear like Paddington about the house in an emergency."

Mr. Brown lay back on his pillow and surveyed the mountain of food on his plate. "Doctor MacAndrew was right about one thing," he said. "While Paddington's looking after us, whatever else happens we certainly shan't starve."

CHAPTER SEVEN

Paddington and the "Finishing Touch"

Mr. Gruber leaned on his shovel and mopped his brow with a large spotted handkerchief. "If anyone had told me three weeks ago, Mr. Brown," he said, "that one day I'd have my own patio in the Portobello Road I wouldn't have believed them.

"In fact," he continued, dusting himself down as he warmed to his subject, "if you hadn't come across that article I might *never* have had one. Now look at it!"

At the sound of Mr. Gruber's voice Paddington rose into view from behind a pile of stones. Lumps of cement clung to his fur like miniature stalactites, his hat was covered in a thin film of grey dust, and his paws — never his strongest point — looked for all the world as if they had been dipped not once but many times into a mixture made up of earth, brickdust and concrete.

All the same, there was a pleased expression on his face as he put down his trowel and hurried across to join his friend near the back door of the shop so that they could inspect the result of their labours.

For in the space of a little over two weeks a great and most remarkable change had come over Mr. Gruber's back yard. A change not unlike that in the transformation scene of a Christmas pantomime.

It had all started when Paddington had come across an article in one of Mrs. Brown's old housekeeping magazines. The article in question had been about the amount of wasted space there was in a big city like London and how, with some thought and a lot of hard work, even the worst rubbish dump could be turned into a place of beauty.

The article had contained a number of photographs showing what could be done and Paddington had been so impressed by these that he'd taken the magazine along to show his friend.

Mr. Gruber kept an antique shop in the Portobello Road and although his back yard wasn't exactly a dumping ground, over the years he had certainly collected a vast amount of rubbish and in the event he'd decided to make a clean sweep of the whole area.

For several days there had been a continual stream of rag and bone men and then soon afterwards builders' lorries became a familiar sight behind the shop as they began to arrive carrying loads of broken paving-stones, sand, gravel, cement, rocks and other items of building material too numerous to be mentioned.

Taking time off each afternoon Mr. Gruber had set about the task of laying the crazy-paving whilst Paddington acted as foreman in charge of cement-mixing and filling the gaps between the stones — a job which he enjoyed no end.

At the far end of the yard Mr. Gruber erected a fence against which he planted some climbing roses and in front of this they built a rockery which was soon filled with various kinds of creeping plants.

In the middle of the patio, space had been left for a small pond containing some goldfish and a miniature fountain, whilst at the house end there now stood a carved wooden seat with room enough for two.

It was on this seat that Paddington and Mr. Gruber relaxed after their exertions each day and finished off any buns which had been left over from their morning elevenses.

"I must say we've been very lucky with the weather," said Mr. Gruber, as Paddington joined him and they took stock of the situation. "It's been a real Indian summer. Though without your help I should never have got it all done before the winter."

Paddington began to look more and more pleased as he sat down on the seat and listened to his friend, for although Mr. Gruber was a polite man, he wasn't in the habit of paying idle compliments.

Mr. Gruber gave a sigh. "If you half close your eyes and listen to the fountain, Mr. Brown," he said, "and then watch all the twinkling lights come on as it begins to get dark, you might be anywhere in the world.

"There's only one thing missing," he continued, after a moment's pause.

Paddington, who'd almost nodded off in order to enjoy a dream in which it was a hot summer's night and he and Mr. Gruber were sipping cocoa under the stars, sat up in surprise.

"What's that, Mr. Gruber?" he asked anxiously, in case he'd left out something important by mistake.

"I don't know," said Mr. Gruber dreamily. "But there's something missing. What the whole thing needs is some kind of finishing touch. A statue or a piece of stonework. I can't think what it can be."

Mr. Gruber gave a shiver as he rose from his seat, for once the sun disappeared over the rooftops a chill came into the air. "We shall just have to put our thinking caps on, Mr. Brown," he said, "and not take them off again until we come up with something. It's a pity to spoil the ship for a ha'p'orth of tar."

"'Adrian Crisp — Garden Ornaments'," exclaimed Mrs. Bird. "What's that bear up to now?" She held up a small piece of paper. "I found this under his bed this morning. It looks as if it's been cut from a magazine. *And my best carrier bag is missing!*"

Mrs. Brown glanced up from her sewing. "I expect it's got something to do with Mr. Gruber's patio," she replied. "Paddington *was* rather quiet when he came in last night. He said he had his thinking cap on and I noticed him poking about looking for my scissors."

Mrs. Bird gave a snort. "That bear's bad enough when he *doesn't* think of things," she said grimly. "There's no knowing what's likely to happen when he really puts his mind to it. Where is he, anyway?"

"I think he went out," said Mrs. Brown vaguely. She took a look at the scrap of paper Mrs. Bird had brought downstairs. "'Works of art in stone bought and sold. No item too small or too large'."

"I don't like the sound of that last bit," broke in Mrs. Bird. "I can see Mr. Gruber ending up with a statue of the Duke of Wellington in his back garden."

"I hope not," said Mrs. Brown. "I can't picture even Paddington trying to get a statue on to a London bus. At least," she added uneasily, "I don't think I can."

Unaware of the detective work going on at number thirty-two Windsor Gardens, Paddington peered around with a confused look on his face. Altogether he was in a bit of a daze. In fact he had to admit that he'd never ever seen anything quite like Mr. Crisp's establishment before.

It occupied a large wilderness of a garden behind a ramshackle old house some distance away from the Browns', and as far as the eye could see every available square inch of ground was covered by statues, seats, pillars, balustrades, posts, stone animals — the list was endless.

Even Adrian Crisp himself, as he followed Paddington in and out of the maze of pathways, seemed to have only a very vague idea of what was actually there.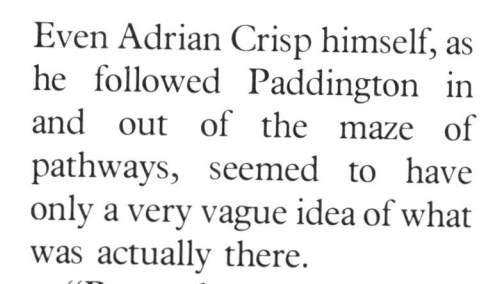

"Pray take your time, my dear chap," he exclaimed, dabbing his face with a silk handkerchief as they reached their starting point for the third time. "Some of these items are hundreds of years old and I think they'll last a while yet. There's no hurry at all."

Paddington thanked Mr. Crisp and then peered thoughtfully at a pair of small stone lions standing near by. They were among the first things he'd seen on entering the garden and all in all they seemed to fit most closely with what he had in mind.

"I think I like the look of those, Mr. Crisp," he exclaimed, bending down in order to undo the secret compartment in his suitcase.

Adrian Crisp followed the direction of Paddington's gaze and then lifted a label attached to one of the lion's ears. "Er...I'm not sure if you'll be able to manage it," he said doubtfully. "The pair are one hundred and seventy pounds."

Paddington remained silent for a moment as he tried to picture the combined weight of one hundred and seventy jars of marmalade. "I quite often bring all Mrs. Bird's shopping home from the market," he said at last.

Adrian Crisp allowed himself a laugh. "Oh, dear me," he said. "I'm afraid we're talking at cross-purposes. That isn't the weight. That's how much they cost."

"One hundred and seventy pounds!" exclaimed Paddington, nearly falling over backwards with surprise.

Mr. Crisp adjusted his bow tie and gave a slight cough as he caught sight of the expression on Paddington's face. "I might be able to let you have a small faun for fifty pounds," he said reluctantly. "I'm afraid the tail's fallen off but it's quite a bargain. If I were to tell you where it came from originally you'd have quite a surprise."

Paddington, who looked as if nothing would surprise him ever again, sat down on his suitcase and stared mournfully at Mr. Crisp.

"I can see you won't be tempted, my dear fellow," said Mr. Crisp, trying to strike a more cheerful note. "Er...how much did you actually think of paying?"

"I was *thinking* of sixpence," said Paddington hopefully.

"*Sixpence!*" If Paddington had been taken by surprise a moment before Adrian Crisp looked positively devastated.

"I could go up to four shillings if I break into my bun money, Mr. Crisp," said Paddington hastily.

"Don't strain your resources too much, bear," said Mr. Crisp delicately removing a lump of leaf mould from his suede shoes. "This isn't a charitable institution, you

know," he continued, eyeing Paddington with disfavour.
"It's been a lifetime's work collecting these items and I
can't let them go for a song."

"I'm afraid I've only got four shillings," said
Paddington firmly.

Adrian Crisp took a deep breath. "I suppose I might be
able to find you one or two bricks," he said sarcastically.
"You'll have to arrange your own transport, of course,
but..." He broke off as he caught Paddington's eye.
Paddington had a very hard stare when he liked and his
present one was certainly one of the most powerful he'd
ever managed.

"Er..." Mr. Crisp glanced round unhappily and then
his face suddenly lit up as he caught sight of something just
behind Paddington. "The very thing!" he exclaimed. "I
could certainly let you have *that* for four shillings."

Paddington turned and looked over his shoulder.
"Thank you very much, Mr. Crisp," he said doubtfully.
"What is it?"

"*What is it?*" Mr. Crisp looked slightly embarrassed. "I
think it fell off something a long time ago," he said hastily.
"I'm not sure what. Anyway, my dear fellow, for four
shillings you don't ask what it is. You should be thankful
for small mercies."

Paddington didn't like to say anything but from where
he was standing Mr. Crisp's object seemed rather a large
mercy. It was big and round and it looked for all the world
like a giant stone football. However, he carefully counted
out his four shillings and handed the money over before

the owner had time to change his mind.

"Thank you, I'm sure," said Mr. Crisp, reluctantly taking possession of a sticky collection of coins made up of several threepenny bits, a number of pennies, and a large pile of ha'pennies. He paused as Paddington turned his attention to the piece of stone. "I shouldn't do that if I were you," he began.

But it was too late. Almost before the words were out of his mouth there came the sound of tearing paper. Paddington stood looking at the two string handles in his paw and then at the sodden remains of brown paper underneath the stone. "That was one of Mrs. Bird's best carrier bags," he exclaimed hotly.

"I did try to warn you, bear," said Mr. Crisp. "You've got a bargain there. That stone's worth five shillings of anybody's money just for the weight alone. If you like to hang on a moment I'll roll it outside for you."

Paddington gave Mr. Crisp a hard stare. "You'll roll it outside for me," he repeated, hardly able to believe his ears. "But I've got to get it all the way back to the Portobello Road."

Mr. Crisp took a deep breath, "I might be able to find you a cardboard box," he said sarcastically, "but I'm afraid we expect you to bring your own string for anything under five shillings."

Mr. Crisp looked as if he'd had enough dealings with bear customers for one day and when, a few minutes later, he ushered Paddington out through the gates he bade him a hasty farewell and slammed the bolts shut on the other side with an air of finality.

Taking a deep breath Paddington placed his suitcase carefully on top of the box, and then clasping the whole lot firmly with both paws, he began staggering up the road in the general direction of Windsor Gardens and the Portobello Road.

If the stone object had seemed large amongst all the other odds and ends in Mr. Crisp's garden, now that he actually had it outside it seemed enormous. Several times he had to stop in order to rest his paws and once, when he accidentally stepped on a grating outside a row of shops, he nearly overbalanced and fell through a window.

Altogether he was thankful when at long last he peered round the side of his load and caught sight of a small queue standing beside a familiar looking London Transport sign not far ahead.

He was only just in time for as he reached the end of the

queue a bus swept to a halt beside the stop and a voice from somewhere upstairs bade everyone to "hurry along."

"Quick," said a man, coming to his rescue, "there's an empty seat up the front."

Before Paddington knew what was happening he found himself being bundled on to the bus whilst several other willing hands in the crowd took charge of the cardboard box for him and placed it in the gangway behind the driver's compartment.

He barely had time to raise his hat in order to thank everyone for their trouble before there was a sudden jerk and the bus set off again on its journey.

Paddington fell back into the seat mopping his brow and as he did so he looked out of the window in some surprise. Although, as far as he could remember, it was a fine day outside, he'd distinctly heard what sounded like the ominous rumble of thunder.

It had seemed quite close for a second or two and he peered anxiously up at the sky in case there was any lightning about, but as far as he could make out there wasn't a cloud anywhere in sight.

At that moment there came a clattering of heavy feet on the stairs as the conductor descended to the bottom deck.

"'Ullo, 'ullo," said a disbelieving voice a second later. "What's all this 'ere?"

Paddington glanced round to see what was going on and as he did so his eyes nearly fell out of their sockets.

The cardboard box, which a moment before had stood neatly and innocently beside him, now had a gaping hole in

107

its side. Worse still, the cause of the hole was now resting at the other end of the gangway!

"Is this yours?" asked the conductor, pointing an accusing finger first at the stone by his feet and then at Paddington.

"I think it must be," said Paddington vaguely.

"Well, I'm not 'aving no bear's boulders on my bus," said the conductor. He indicated a notice just above his head. "It says 'ere plain enough — 'parcels may be left under the staircase by permission of the conductor' — and I ain't given me permission. Nor likely to neither. Landed on me best corn it did."

"It isn't a bear's boulder," exclaimed Paddington hotly. "It's Mr. Gruber's 'finishing touch'."

The conductor reached up and rang the bell. "It'll be your finishing touch and all if I have any more nonsense," he said crossly. "Come on — off with you."

The conductor looked as if he'd been about to say a great deal more on the subject of bear passengers in general and Paddington and his piece of stonework in particular when he suddenly broke off. For as the bus ground to a halt the stone suddenly began trundling back up the gangway, ending its journey with a loud bang against the wall at the driver's end.

A rather cross-looking face appeared for a moment at the window just above it. Then the bus surged forward again and before anyone had time to stop it the stone began rolling back down the gangway, landing once more at the conductor's feet.

"I've 'ad just about enough of this!" he exclaimed, hopping up and down as he reached for the bell. "We've gone past two requests and a compulsory as it is."

The words were hardly out of his mouth when a by now familiar thundering noise followed by an equally familiar thump drowned the excited conversation from the other passengers in the bus.

For a moment or two the bus seemed to hover shaking in mid-air as if one half wanted to go on and the other half wanted to stay. Then, with a screech of brakes, it pulled in to the side of the road and as it ground to a halt the driver jumped out and came hurrying round to the back.

"Why don't you make up your mind?" he cried, addressing his mate on the platform. "First you rings the bell to say you want to stop. Then you bangs on me panel to say go on. Then you rings the bell again. Then it's bang on me panel. I don't know whether I'm on me head or me heels, let alone driving a bus."

"I like that!" exclaimed the conductor. "*I* banged on your panel. It was that blessed bear with 'is boulder what done it."

"A bear with a boulder?" repeated the driver disbelievingly. "Where? I can't see him."

The conductor looked up the gangway and then his face turned white. "He *was* there," he said. "And he had this boulder what kept rolling up and down the gangway."

"There he is!" he exclaimed triumphantly. "I told you so!"

He pointed down the road to where in the distance a

small brown figure could be seen hurrying after a round, grey object as it zigzagged down the road. "It must have fallen off the last time you stopped."

"Well, I hope he catches it before it gets to the Portobello Road," said the driver. "If it gets in amongst all them barrows there's no knowing what'll happen."

"Bears!" exclaimed the conductor bitterly, as a sudden thought struck him. "He didn't even pay for 'is fare let alone extra for 'is boulder."

Paddington and Mr. Gruber settled themselves comfortably on the patio seat. After all his exertions in the early part of the day Paddington was glad of a rest and the sight of a tray laden with two mugs, a jug of cocoa and a plate of buns into the bargain was doubly welcome.

Mr. Gruber had been quite overwhelmed when Paddington presented him with the piece of stone.

"I don't know when I've had such a nice present, Mr. Brown," he said. "Or such an unexpected one. How you managed to get it all the way here by yourself I really don't know."

"It was rather heavy, Mr. Gruber," admitted Paddington. "I nearly strained my resources."

"Fancy that conductor calling it a boulder," continued Mr. Gruber, looking at the stone with a thoughtful expression on his face.

"Even Mr. Crisp didn't seem to know quite what it was," said Paddington. "But he said it was a very good bargain."

"I'm sure he was right," agreed Mr. Gruber. He examined the top of the stone carefully and ran his fingers over the top, which appeared to have a flatter surface than the rest and was surrounded by a rim, not unlike a small tray. "Do you know what I think it is, Mr. Brown?"

Paddington shook his head.

"I think it's an old Roman cocoa stand," said Mr. Gruber.

"A Roman cocoa stand," repeated Paddington excitedly.

"Well, perhaps it isn't exactly Roman," replied Mr. Gruber truthfully. "But it's certainly very old and I can't think of a better use for it."

He reached over for the jug, filled both mugs to the brim with steaming liquid and then carefully placed them on top of the stone. To Paddington's surprise they fitted exactly.

"There," said Mr. Gruber with obvious pleasure. "I don't think anyone could find a better finishing touch for their patio than that, Mr. Brown. Not if they tried for a thousand years."

CHAPTER EIGHT

Paddington Steps Out

Mrs. Brown looked out of the car window. "If you want my opinion," she said, lowering her voice so that the occupants of the back seat, and one occupant in particular, shouldn't hear, "bringing Paddington with us is asking for trouble. You know what happened when he went to Jonathan's school."

"That wasn't exactly a disaster," said Mr. Brown mildly. "If I remember rightly he saved the day. If it hadn't been for him the old boys would never have won their cricket match."

"Playing in a cricket match isn't the same as watching ballet," replied Mrs. Brown. "He'll never sit quietly through a whole afternoon of it. Something's bound to happen."

She gave a sigh. Ever since Paddington had taken part in an epic cricket match at Jonathan's school, Judy had been clamouring for him to visit her school in turn and Mrs. Brown knew that she was fighting a losing battle.

Having a bear in the family gave both Jonathan and Judy a certain amount of prestige amongst their fellow pupils and Judy was anxious to catch up on the lead at present held by her brother. All the same, as they drew nearer and nearer to Judy's school, Mrs. Brown began to look more and more worried.

"Good heavens!" exclaimed Mr. Brown suddenly as they turned a corner and passed through some wrought iron gates let into a grey stone wall. He waved his hand towards a seething mass of girls in uniform as he brought the car to a halt. "What's this — some sort of reception committee?"

"What did I tell you?" said Mrs. Brown, as the familiar figure of Judy detached itself from the crowd and came forward to greet them. "It's started already."

"Nonsense!" said Mr. Brown. All the same he cast some anxious glances towards the paintwork on his car as he helped the others out and exchanged greetings with his daughter.

Paddington, as he clambered out of the back seat, looked even more surprised as he stood blinking in the strong sunlight listening to the cheers, and he raised his hat several times in response to the cries.

"Come along, Paddington," said Judy, grabbing his paw. "You've lots of people to meet *and* we've got to pay a visit to the tuck shop. I told Mrs. Beedle, the lady in charge, all about you and she's laid on some special marmalade sandwiches."

"Mrs. Beedle's laid on some marmalade sandwiches!" exclaimed Paddington, looking most impressed. Although he was very keen on anything to do with marmalade and had several times sat on a sandwich by mistake he'd never met anyone who'd actually done it on purpose before, particularly someone in charge of a tuck shop. However, before he had time to inquire into the matter the throng of girls closed in behind him and he felt himself being propelled gently but firmly in the direction of a small building which stood to one side of the quadrangle in front of the main block.

As the milling crowd of figures disappeared through the door of the tuck shop, Mrs. Brown looked towards a large, brightly coloured poster on a board near the main gate. "I thought this Russian dancer they're having down — Sergei Oblomov — was supposed to be the guest of honour," she remarked. "I don't think he'll like it if he turns up and there's no one here. I'm sure all these girls were meant for him, not Paddington."

"Talk of the devil," said Mr. Brown, as a large, important looking black car swept in through the gates and came to a halt a few yards away. "I have a feeling this *is* him."

Pretending to study the scenery, the Browns nevertheless

watched with interest as the door of the car opened and a tall figure dressed in a black cloak alighted and stood for a moment with one hand in the air looking expectantly all around.

"Crikey!" said Jonathan a few moments later as the sound of a door being slammed echoed round the quadrangle and the car swept past them in a cloud of dust towards the school building. "He didn't look in a very good mood."

"Black as ink," agreed Mr. Brown. "It wasn't exactly what you might call a good entrance. Not so much as a pigeon cooed."

"I don't suppose you'd like it," said Mrs. Brown, "if you were a famous dancer and you had your thunder stolen by a bear. Especially one stuffing himself with marmalade sandwiches in a school tuck shop."

"He doesn't know it's a bear," reasoned Mr. Brown. "He's never even met Paddington."

"No," said Mrs. Brown decidedly, as they made their way towards the school buildings, "he hasn't. And if I have my way he's not going to either."

She cast some anxious glances in the direction of the tuck shop as they passed by. Several times the ominous sound of cheering had come from the open windows and one or two of them had been decidedly loud, rather as if things were getting out of control.

All the same, as they seated themselves in the school hall some while later, even Mrs. Brown found it hard to fault Paddington's appearance. Admittedly there were still one or two traces of marmalade on his whiskers and his fur had lost some of its smooth sheen, but all in all he looked unusually well behaved as he settled himself at the end of the row by the gangway and examined his programme with interest.

"You know, I'm really looking forward to this," said Mrs. Bird with enthusiasm, as she made herself comfortable. "I like ballet dancing."

The others looked at their housekeeper in surprise as a far-away look came into her eyes. "I haven't seen any good dancing for I don't know how many years."

"I'm not sure you're going to now," whispered Mr. Brown, as the curtain rose to reveal a woodland glade and several small figures dressed as toadstools.

"It's the Juniors," whispered Judy. "They're doing their 'nature' dance."

Paddington opened his suitcase, took out his opera glasses, and peered at the stage with interest.

"Are you enjoying it?" whispered Judy.

Paddington thought for a moment. "It's all right," he announced after some thought. "But I can't hear what they're saying."

"People don't *say* anything in ballet," hissed Judy. "They mime it all. You have to guesss what they're doing by the dancing."

Paddington sank back into his seat. Although he didn't want to hurt Judy's feelings by saying so, he didn't think much of ballet at all. As far as he could see it was just a lot of people running after each other on the stage, and apart from not saying anything, which made it all rather difficult to follow, he began to wonder why they didn't get taller dancers in the first place as some of the older girls in particular seemed to spend most of the time standing on their toes. However, he was a polite bear and he applauded dutifully at the end of each item.

"I must say that swan took a long time to die," said Mr. Brown, as the lights went up at long last to herald the interval. "I thought she was never going to get it over with."

"I liked the flying ballet," said Mrs. Brown, amid general agreement. "I thought that was very well done."

"I'd like to go up in the air on a wire like that," said Jonathan. "I bet it's super."

Judy handed Paddington her programme. "It's the famous Russian dancer next," she said. "Look — there's his picture."

Paddington peered at the programme with interest. "Surge Oblomov!" he exclaimed in surprise.

"It's not *Surge,*" said Judy. "It's pronounced Sur-guy."

"Sir Guy Oblomov," repeated Paddington, looking most impressed as he studied the picture. "I don't think I've ever seen a Lord doing a ballet dance before."

"He isn't a Lord — he's a..." Judy gave a sigh as she sought for the right words. Sometimes explaining things to Paddington became complicated out of all proportion.

"Well, whatever he is," said Mrs. Bird, coming to her rescue, "I'm really looking forward to it. It's a great treat."

"Oh, crikey!" exclaimed Judy suddenly, as a girl from the row behind whispered something in her ear. "I'm not sure if he's going to appear after all. They're having some trouble back stage."

"What!" exclaimed Paddington hotly. "Sir Guy Oblomov's not going to appear!"

"Oh, dear," said Mrs. Bird. "How very disappointing."

Paddington stared at the drawn curtains on the stage hardly able to believe his ears as everyone began talking at once. Judy's words had reached several other people nearby and soon a buzz of excitement went round the hall.

"It's something to do with no one being at the gates to meet him," explained the girl in the seat behind. "He's a bit temperamental and it upset him rather."

118

Mr. and Mrs. Brown exchanged glances. "I told you so, Henry," said Mrs. Brown. "I said if we brought Paddington something would happen."

"Well, you can't really blame poor old Paddington for this," replied Mr. Brown indignantly. "It's not his fault if everyone wanted to meet him instead of some blessed ballet dancer chap. After all..." Mr. Brown suddenly broke off in mid-sentence. "That's funny," he said, as he looked along the aisle. "Talking of Paddington, where's he got to?"

"He was here a second ago," said Judy, looking all around.

"Look!" cried Jonathan, pointing down the aisle. "There he is!"

The Browns followed the direction of Jonathan's arm and were just in time to see a small figure disappear through a door at the side of the stage. From where they were sitting it wasn't possible to see the expression on Paddington's face but there was a determined slant to his hat and a look about his duffle coat which seemed to bode ill for anyone who got in his way.

"Don't you think you'd better go after him, Judy?" said Mrs. Brown anxiously.

"Too late," groaned Judy. "Did you see who was behind the door? Miss Grimshaw!"

Judy sank lower and lower into her seat as she contemplated the awful prospect of Paddington coming face to face with her headmistress, although had she but known, Miss Grimshaw, weighed down by all the worries back stage, seemed almost glad to find someone from outside the school she could talk to.

"Are you Russian?" she asked hopefully, after Paddington had introduced himself.

"Well, I am in a bit of a hurry," admitted Paddington, raising his hat politely. "I've come to see Sir Guy."

Miss Grimshaw looked at him suspiciously. "I said 'Russian'," she explained. "Not *rushing*. And I'm not at all sure Mr. Oblomov will see you. I was hoping you might be Russian so that you could talk to him in his own language and make him feel more at home, but if you're not I'd rather you didn't."

"Mrs. Bird's very upset," replied Paddington.

"I'm sure she is," said Miss Grimshaw. "We're all upset. Mr. Oblomov's upset. Deirdre Shaw's upset."

"*Deirdre Shaw?*" echoed Paddington, looking most surprised.

"She was supposed to partner Mr. Oblomov in the *Pas de deux*," explained Miss Grimshaw. "Then when Mr. Oblomov said he wouldn't dance she ran off to her dormitory in tears and no one's seen her since."

While Miss Grimshaw was speaking, a nearby door opened and a tall, imposing figure in black tights emerged.

"I hov changed my mind," announced Mr. Oblomov, waving his hand imperiously as he did a series of knee-bending exercises. "I will not disappoint my public. First I will dance my famous solo from the Swan Lake. Then I will perform the *Pas de deux*. I trust everything is ready, no?"

"No," exclaimed Miss Grimshaw. "I mean...that is to say...yes. I'm sure it will be."

Miss Grimshaw's usual icy calm seemed to have deserted her for once as Sergei Oblomov strode past heading for the stage.

"Oh, dear," she exclaimed. "Now he's changed his mind *again* — and Deirdre Shaw's disappeared. What he's going to say when he finds he's without a partner in the second half I shudder to think."

As the school orchestra started up and the curtain rose to a tremendous round of applause, Miss Grimshaw rushed off wringing her hands, leaving Paddington staring, with a very thoughtful expression on his face indeed, in the direction of the open door leading to Sergei Oblomov's dressing-room.

It was an expression that the Browns, had they been there, would have recognised immediately. But fortunately for their peace of mind they, like practically everyone else in the school, had their attention riveted to the stage.

Even Mr. Brown sat up in his seat and clapped as loudly as anyone as Sergei Oblomov executed one perfect pirouette after another, spinning round and round so fast it left the audience breathless. And when he followed this with a series of breathtaking arabesques everyone gasped with admiration and the rafters of the hall fairly shook with the ovation which greeted the end of this item.

As the applause died away and Sergei Oblomov stood for a moment motionless in the beam from a single spotlight, Mrs. Bird gave a quick glance at her programme.

"It's the *Pas de deux* now," she whispered.

"Golly, I hope they've found Deirdre Shaw," said Judy in a low voice as the music started up. "There's going to be an awful row if they haven't."

"It's all right," said Mr. Brown. "I think I can see someone lurking at the side of the stage."

Judy followed the direction of Mr. Brown's gaze and then jumped up from her seat in alarm.

"Crikey!" she exclaimed. "That's not Deirdre Shaw. That's..."

"Paddington!" exclaimed the rest of the family, joining her in a chorus as the shadowy figure moved on to the stage and into the light.

"Mercy me!" cried Mrs. Bird. "What on earth is that bear up to now?"

Her words were lost in the gasp of astonishment which went up all around them as Paddington advanced towards the centre of the stage, placed his suitcase carefully in front of the footlights, and then raised his hat politely to the several members of the audience in the front row who began half-heartedly to applaud.

"Oh, dear, I wish he wouldn't wear that old hat," said Mrs. Brown.

"And what on earth's he got on his legs?" asked Mrs. Bird.

"Looks like some kind of sacking to me," said Mr. Brown.

"They're not sacks," said Judy. "They're tights."

"Tights?" echoed Mr. Brown. "They don't look very

tight to me. They look as if they're going to come down any moment."

The Browns watched in horror as Paddington, having ventured one bow too many, hurriedly replaced his hat and grabbed hold of the roll of material which hung around his waist in large folds.

Now, for the first time since he'd decided to lend a paw with the ballet, he was beginning to wish he'd resisted the temptation to use the pair of tights which he'd found hanging on the back of Mr. Oblomov's dressing-room door.

Bears' legs being rather short put him at a disadvantage to start with, but as far as he could make out Sergei Oblomov's legs were twice as long as anyone else's so that an unusually large amount of surplus material had to be lost at the top.

Apart from tying a piece of string round his waist Paddington had hopefully made use of several drawing pins which he'd found on a notice board at the back of the stage, but most of these seemed to have fallen out so he had to spend some moments making last minute adjustments to a large safety pin which he'd put on in case of an emergency.

It was at this moment that Sergei Oblomov, oblivious to all that had been going on, finished executing a particularly long and difficult pirouette near a pillar at the back of the stage and came hurrying down towards him.

He stood for a moment poised on one foot, his eyes closed as he prepared himself for the big moment.

Paddington raised his hat politely once again and then took hold of one of Mr. Oblomov's outstretched hands and shook it warmly with his paw.

"Good afternoon, Sir Guy," he exclaimed. "I've come to do the *Pas de deux.*"

Sergei Oblomov seemed suddenly to freeze in his position. For a brief moment, in fact, he seemed almost to have turned into stone and Paddington looked at him rather anxiously, but then several things happened to him in quick succession.

First he opened his eyes, then he closed them and a shiver passed through his body, starting at his toes and travelling up to his head, almost as if he had been shot. Then he opened his eyes again and stared distastefully at his hand. It was warm under the lights and some kind of sticky substance seemed to have transferred itself from

Paddington's paw.

"It's all right, Sir Guy," explained Paddington, wiping his paw hastily on one of the folds in his tights. "It's only marmalade. I forgot to wash it off when I came out of the tuck shop."

If Mr. Oblomov knew what marmalade was or, for that matter, if he'd ever heard of a tuck shop, he gave no sign. A shiver again seemed to pass through his body and as the music reached a crescendo he closed his eyes and with a supreme effort prepared himself once more for the *Pas de deux*.

Feeling very pleased that things seemed to have turned out all right in the end Paddington took hold of Sergei Oblomov's outstretched hand and bent down to pick up his suitcase.

The next moment it felt as if he was in the centre of an earthquake, a tornado and a barrage of thunderbolts all rolled into one.

First it seemed as if his arm had been torn out of its socket, then he felt himself spinning round and round like a top; finally he landed, still spinning, in a heap on the floor of the stage some distance away from Mr. Oblomov.

For a moment he lay where he was gasping for breath and then he struggled to his feet just in time to see a vague figure in tights heading towards him through the glare of the footlights. As he focused on the scene Paddington noticed a nasty looking gleam in Sergei Oblomov's eyes which he didn't like the look of at all and so he hurriedly sat down again.

Mr. Oblomov came to a halt and stared down at the figure on the floor. "I cannot go on," he exclaimed gloomily. "For one zing you hov too much shortness — and for zee second thing — your *entrechats* — zey are not clean."

"My *entrechats* are not clean!" exclaimed Paddington hotly. "But I had a bath last night."

"I do not mean zey are dirty," hissed Mr. Oblomov. "I mean zey should be clean — snappy — like so!"

Without further ado he threw himself into the air, beat his legs together, crossed them in time to the music, and then uncrossed them again as he landed gracefully on one foot facing the audience.

Paddington looked rather doubtful as the applause rang through the hall. "It's a bit difficult when you've only got paws, Sir Guy," he exclaimed. "But I'll have a try."

Closing his eyes as he'd seen Mr. Oblomov do, Paddington jumped into the air, made a half-hearted attempt to cross his legs and then, as his tights began to slip, landed rather heavily on the stage. As he did so, to everyone's surprise he suddenly shot up into the air again, his legs crossing and uncrossing, almost as if he'd been

126

fired from a cannon.

"Good gracious!" exclaimed someone near the Browns, "that young bear's done a triple!"

"A sixer," contradicted another elderly gentleman knowledgeably, as Paddington landed and then shot up in the air again with a loud cry. "Bravo!" he called, trying to make himself heard above the applause.

Even Sergei Oblomov began to look impressed as Paddington executed several more *entrechats* each one higher and more complicated than the one before. Then, to show he wasn't beaten, he himself gave a tremendous leap into the air, changed his legs over, beat them together, changed them back again, beat them together once more, and then, to a roar from the audience crossed them once again before landing.

Paddington, who had been spending the last few seconds sitting on the stage peering at one of his paws jumped up with a loud cry which echoed round the rafters as Sergei Oblomov landed heavily on his other paw.

If the applause for Sergei Oblomov's *entrechat* had been loud it was nothing compared to that which greeted Paddington as he shot up into the air once more, waving his paws wildly to and fro, crossing and uncrossing them and bringing them together before he landed and then catapulted up again almost out of sight.

This time Sergei Oblomov himself had to acknowledge he'd met his match and with a graceful bow which brought murmurs of approval from the audience he stood back and joined in the applause as the music finally came to an end, and with Paddington's leaps growing higher and wilder with every passing second the curtain came down.

"Well," said Mr. Brown as the applause finally subsided. "It may not have been the best ballet I've ever seen but it was certainly the most exciting."

"Haven't seen anything like it since the Cossacks," agreed the elderly gentleman nearby. "Five Grand Royales in a row!"

Thoroughly surprised by the events of the afternoon the Browns tried to make their way back stage, but what with the speeches and the crowds of girls who came up to Judy in order to congratulate her on Paddington's performance, it was some while before they were able to force their way through the door at the side of the stage. When they did finally break through they were even more surprised to find that Paddington had been removed to the school sanatorium for what was called "urgent First Aid."

"Oh, dear, I hope he hasn't broken anything," said Mrs. Brown anxiously as they hurried across the quadrangle. "Some of those jumps he did were very high."

"More likely to have slipped on a marmalade chunk," said Mrs. Bird darkly as they hurried into the ward. But even Mrs. Bird looked worried when she caught sight of Paddington lying on a bed with his two back paws sticking up in the air swathed in bandages.

"I can't understand it," said Miss Grimshaw, as she came forward to greet them. "Both his back paws are full of holes. I really must find matron and see what she's got to say."

"Holes?" echoed the Browns.

"Holes," said Miss Grimshaw. "Quite small ones. Almost as if he's got woodworm. Not that he could have of course," she added hastily as a groan came from the direction of the bed.

"Such a shame after the magnificent performance he gave. I doubt if we shall see the like again."

As Miss Grimshaw hurried off in search of the matron Mrs. Bird gave a snort. Something about Paddington's leaps on the stage had aroused her suspicions and now her eagle eyes had spotted a number of small shiny objects under the bed that so far no one else had seen.

"Bears who try to pin their tights up with drawing pins," she said sternly, "mustn't be surprised when they fall out. And," she added, "they musn't be disappointed if they step on them into the bargain and have to stay in hospital and miss the special marmalade pudding that's waiting for them at home."

Paddington sat up in bed. "I think perhaps they're getting better now," he said hastily.

Being an invalid with everyone fussing around was rather nice. On the other hand, marmalade pudding, particularly Mrs. Bird's marmalade pudding, was even nicer.

"But it's no good if you want to carry on dancing," warned Mrs. Bird, as he clambered out of bed and tested his paws on the floor. "It's much too rich and heavy. In fact, I'm not sure that you oughtn't to go on a diet."

But Mrs. Bird's words fell on empty air as Paddington disappeared through the door in the direction of the car with remarkable haste for one who'd only just risen from a sick bed.

"Perhaps it's as well," said Mr. Brown gravely, as the others followed. "I can't really picture Paddington embarking on a career as a ballet dancer."

"All those exercises," agreed Mrs. Brown with a shudder.

"And those tights," said Judy.

"And all that leaping about," added Mrs. Bird. "If you ask me it's much better to be simply a bear who likes his marmalade."

"Especially," said Jonathan, amid general agreement, "if you happen to be a bear called Paddington."

CHAPTER NINE

Paddington and the "Cold Snap"

Paddington stood on the front door step of number thirty-two Windsor Gardens and sniffed the morning air. He peered out through the gap between his duffle coat hood and a brightly coloured scarf which was wound tightly about his neck.

On the little that could be seen of his face behind some unusually white-looking whiskers there was a mixture of surprise and excitement as he took in the sight which met his eyes.

Overnight a great change had come over the weather. Whereas the day before had been mild, almost springlike for early January, now everything was covered by a thick white blanket of snow which reached almost to the top of his Wellington boots.

Not a sound disturbed the morning air. Apart from the clatter of breakfast things in the kitchen, where Mrs. Brown and Mrs. Bird were busy washing up, the only sign that he wasn't alone in the world came from a row of milk bottle tops poking through the snow on the step and a long trail of footprints where the postman had been earlier that day.

Paddington liked snow, but as he gazed at the view in the street outside he almost agreed with Mrs. Bird, the Browns' housekeeper, that it was possible to have too much of a good thing. Since he'd been living with the Brown family there had been several of Mrs. Bird's "cold snaps", but he couldn't remember ever seeing one before in which the snow had settled quite so deep and crisp and evenly.

All the same, Paddington wasn't the sort of bear to waste a good opportunity and a moment or so later he closed the door behind him and made his way down the side of the house as quickly as he could in order to investigate the matter. Apart from the prospect of playing snowballs he was particularly anxious to test his new Wellingtons which had been standing in his bedroom waiting for just such a moment ever since Mrs. Brown had given them to him at Christmas.

After he reached Mr. Brown's cabbage patch Paddington busied himself scooping the snow up with his paws and rolling it into firm round balls which he threw at the clothes post. But after several of the larger ones narrowly missed hitting the next-door greenhouse instead, he hastily turned his attention to the more important task of building a snowman and gradually peace returned once again to Windsor Gardens.

It was some while later, just as he was adding the finishing touches to the snowman's head with some old lemonade bottle tops, that the quiet was suddenly shattered by the sound of a nearby window being flung open.

"Bear!" came a loud voice. "Is that you, bear?"

Paddington jumped in alarm as he lifted his duffle coat hood and caught sight of the Browns' next door neighbour leaning out of his bedroom window. Mr. Curry was dressed in pyjamas and a dressing gown and half of his face seemed to be hidden behind a large white handkerchief.

"I've finished throwing snowballs, Mr. Curry," explained Paddington hastily. "I'm making a snowman instead."

To his surprise Mr. Curry looked unusually friendly as he lifted the handkerchief from his face. "That's all right, bear," he called in a mild tone of voice. "I wasn't grumbling. I just wondered if you would care to do me a small favour and earn yourself sixpence bun money into the bargain.

"I've caught a nasty cold in my dose," he continued, as Paddington climbed up on a box and peered over the fence.

"A cold in your *dose*, Mr. Curry," repeated Paddington, looking most surprised. He had never heard of anyone having a cold in their dose before and he stared up at the window with interest.

Mr. Curry took a deep breath. "Not *dose*," he said, swallowing hard and making a great effort. "*Dnose*. And as if that isn't enough, my system is frozen."

Paddington became more and more upset as he listened to Mr. Curry and he nearly fell off his box with alarm at the last piece of information. "Your system's frozen!" he exclaimed. "I'll ask Mrs. Bird to send for Doctor MacAndrew."

Mr. Curry snorted. "I don't want a doctor, bear," he said crossly. "I want a plumber. It's not my own pipes that are frozen. It's the water pipes. There isn't even enough left in the tank to fill my hot-water bottle."

Paddington looked slightly disappointed as a heavy object wrapped in a piece of paper landed at his feet.

"That's my front door key," explained Mr. Curry. "I want you to take it along to Mr. James, the odd job man.

Tell him he's to come at once. I shall be in bed but he can let himself in. And tell him not to make too much noise — I may be asleep. And no hanging about round the bun shop on the way otherwise you won't get your sixpence."

With that Mr. Curry blew his nose violently several times and slammed his window shut.

Mr. Curry was well known in the neighbourhood for his meanness. He had a habit of promising people a reward for running his errands but somehow whenever the time for payment arrived he was never to be found. Paddington had a nasty feeling in the back of his mind that this was going to be one of those occasions and he stood staring up at the empty window for some moments before he turned and made his way slowly in the direction of Mr. James's house.

"Curry!" exclaimed Mr. James, as he stood in his doorway and stared down at Paddington. "Did you say Curry?"

"That's right, Mr. James," said Paddington, raising his duffle coat hood politely. "His system's frozen and he can't even fill his hot-water bottle."

"Hard luck," said the odd job man unsympathetically. "I'm having enough trouble with me own pipes this morning let alone that there Mr. Curry's. Besides, I know him and his little jobs. He hasn't paid me yet for the last one I did — and that was six months ago. Tell him from me, I want to see the colour of his money before I do anything else and even then I'll have to think twice."

Paddington looked most disappointed as he listened to Mr. James. From the little he could remember of Mr.

Curry's money it was usually a very dirty colour as if it had been kept under lock and key for a long time, and he felt sure Mr. James would be even less keen on doing any jobs if he saw it.

"Tell you what," said the odd job man, relenting slightly as he caught sight of the expression on Paddington's face. "Hang on a tick. Seeing you've come a long way in the snow, I'll see what I can do to oblige."

Mr. James disappeared from view only to return a moment later carrying a large brown paper parcel. "I'm lending Mr. Curry a blowlamp," he explained. "And I've slipped in a book on plumbing as well. He might find a few tips in it if he gets stuck."

"A blowlamp!" exclaimed Paddington, his eyes growing larger and larger. "I don't think he'll like that very much."

"You can take it or leave it," said Mr. James. "It's all the same to me. But if you want my advice, bear, you'll take it. This weather's going to get a lot worse before it gets any better."

So saying, Mr. James bade a final good morning and closed his door firmly, leaving Paddington standing on the step with a very worried expression on his face as he stared down at the parcel in his paws.

Mr. Curry didn't have a very good temper at the best of times and the thought of waking him in order to hand over a blowlamp or even a book on plumbing, especially when he had a bad cold, filled him with alarm.

Paddington's face grew longer and longer the more he thought about it, but by the time he turned to make his way back to Windsor Gardens his whiskers were so well covered by flakes that only the closest passer by would have noticed anything amiss.

Mrs. Brown paused in her housework as a small figure hurried past the kitchen window. "I suppose," she said with a sigh, "we can look forward to paw prints all over the house for the next few days."

"If this weather keeps on that bear'll have to watch more than his paws," said Mrs. Bird as she joined her. "He'll have to mind his p's and q's as well."

The Browns' housekeeper held very strict views on the subject of dirty floors, particularly when they were the result of bears' "goings on" in the snow, and she followed Paddington's progress into Mr. Brown's garage with a disapproving look.

"I think he must be helping out next door," said Mrs. Brown as Paddington came into view again clutching something beneath his duffle coat. "It sounds as if Mr. Curry's having trouble with his pipes."

"I hope that's all he's having trouble with," said Mrs. Bird. "There's been far too much hurrying about this morning for my liking."

Mrs. Bird was never very happy when Paddington helped out and several times she'd caught sight of him going past the kitchen window with what looked suspiciously like pieces of old piping sticking out of his duffle coat.

Even as she spoke a renewed burst of hammering came

from the direction of Mr. Curry's bathroom and echoed round the space between the two houses. First there were one or two bangs, then a whole series which grew louder and louder, finally ending in a loud crash and a period of silence broken only by the steady hiss of a blowlamp.

"If it sounds like that in here," said Mrs. Brown, "goodness only knows what it must be like next door."

"It isn't what it sounds like," replied Mrs. Bird grimly, "it's what it looks like that worries me."

The Browns' housekeeper left the window and began busying herself at the stove. Mrs. Bird was a great believer in letting people get on with their own work and the activities of Mr. Curry's plumber were no concern of hers. All the same, had she waited a moment longer she might have changed her views on the matter, for at that moment the window of Mr. Curry's bathroom opened and a familiar looking hat followed by some equally familiar whiskers came into view.

From the expression on his face as he leant over the sill and peered at the ground far below it looked very much as if Paddington would have been the first to agree with Mrs. Bird's remarks on the subject.

Paddington was an optimistic bear at heart but as he clambered back down from the window and viewed Mr. Curry's bathroom even he had to admit to himself that things were in a bit of a mess. In fact, taking things all round he was beginning to wish he'd never started on the job in the first place.

Apart from Mr. James's blowlamp and a large number of tools from Mr. Brown's garage, the floor was strewn with odd lengths of pipe, pieces of solder and several saucepans, not to mention a length of hosepipe which he'd brought up from the garden in case of an emergency.

But it wasn't so much the general clutter that caused Paddington's gloomy expression as the amount of water which lay everywhere. In fact, considering the pipes had been completely frozen when he'd started, he found it hard to understand where it had all come from. The only place in the whole of the bathroom where there wasn't some kind of pool was in a corner by the washbasin where he'd placed one of his Wellington boots beneath a leaking pipe in the hope of getting enough water to fill Mr. Curry's hotwater bottle.

Paddington was particularly anxious to fill the bottle before Mr. Curry took it into his head to get up. Already there had been several signs of stirring from the direction of his bedroom and twice a loud voice had called out demanding to know what was going on. Both times Paddington had done his best to make a deep grunting noise like a plumber hard at work and each time Mr. Curry's voice had grown more suspicious.

Paddington hastily began scooping water off the floor with his paw in order to help matters along, but as fast as he scooped the water up it soaked into his fur and ran back up his arm. Hopefully squeezing a few drops from his elbow into the Wellington boot Paddington gave a deep sigh and turned his attention to the book Mr. James had lent him.

The book was called *The Plumber's Mate* by Bert Stilson, and although Paddington felt sure it was very good for anyone who wanted to fit pipes in their house for the first time there didn't seem to be a great deal on what to do once they were in and frozen hard. Mr. Stilson seemed to be unusually lucky with the weather whenever he did a job, for in nearly all the photographs it was possible to see the sun shining through the open windows.

There was only one chapter on frozen pipes and in the picture that went with it Mr. Stilson was shown wrapping them in towels soaked in boiling water. With no water to boil Paddington had tried holding Mr. Curry's one and only towel near the blowlamp in order to warm it, but after several rather nasty brown patches suddenly appeared he'd hastily given it up as a bad job.

Another picture showed Mr. Stilson playing the flame of a blowlamp along a pipe as he dealt with a particularly difficult job and Paddington had found this method much more successful. The only trouble was that as soon as the ice inside the pipe began to melt a leak appeared near one of the joints.

Paddington tried stopping the leak with his paw while he read to the end of the chapter, but on the subject of

140

leaking pipes Mr. Stilson was even less helpful than he had been on frozen ones. In a note about lead pipes he mentioned hitting them with a hammer in order to close the gap, but whenever Paddington hit one of Mr. Curry's gaps at least one other leak appeared farther along the pipe so that instead of the one he'd started with there were now five and he'd run out of paws.

For some while the quiet of the bathroom was broken only by the hiss of the blowlamp and the steady drip, drip, drip of water as Paddington sat lost in thought.

Suddenly, as he turned over a page near the end of the book his face brightened. Right at the end of the very last chapter Mr. Stilson had drawn out a chart which he'd labelled "Likely Trouble Spots". Hurriedly unfolding the paper Paddington spread it over the bathroom stool and began studying it with interest.

According to Mr. Stilson most things to do with plumbing caused trouble at some time or another, but if there was one place which was more troublesome than all the others put together it was where there was a bend in the pipe. At the bottom of the chart Mr. Stilson explained that bends shaped like the letter "U" always had water inside them and so they were the very first places to freeze when the cold weather came.

Looking around Mr. Curry's bathroom Paddington was surprised to see how many "U" bends there were. In fact, wherever he looked there appeared to be a bend of one kind or another.

Holding Mr. Stilson's book in one paw Paddington

picked up the blowlamp in the other and settled himself underneath the washbasin where one of the pipes made itself into a particularly large "U" shape before it entered the cold tap.

As he played the flame along the pipe, sitting well back in case he accidentally singed his whiskers, Paddington was pleased to hear several small cracking noises coming from somewhere inside. In a matter of moments the crackles were replaced by bangs, and his opinion of Mr. Stilson went up by leaps and bounds as almost immediately afterwards a loud gurgling sound came from the basin over his head and the water began to flow.

To make doubly sure of matters Paddington stood up and ran the blowlamp flame along the pipe with one final sweep of his paw. It was as he did so that the pleased expression on his face suddenly froze almost as solidly as the water in Mr. Curry's pipes had been a second before.

Everything happened so quickly it all seemed to be over in the blink of an eyelid, but one moment he was standing under the basin with the blowlamp, the next moment there was a hiss and loud plop and before his astonished gaze Mr. Curry's "U" bend disappeared into thin air. Paddington just had time to take in the pool of molten lead on the bathroom floor before a gush of cold water hit him on the chin, nearly bowling him over.

Acting with great presence of mind he knocked the hot flexible remains of the pipe and turned it back into Mr. Curry's bath, leaving the water to hiss and gurgle as he turned to consult Mr. Stilson's book once more. There was

142

a note somewhere near the back telling what to do in cases of emergency which he was particularly anxious to read.

A few seconds later he hurried downstairs as fast as his legs would carry him, slamming the front door in his haste. Almost at the same moment as it banged shut there came the sound of a window being opened somewhere overhead and Mr. Curry's voice rang out. "Bear!" he roared. "What's going on, bear?"

Paddington gazed wildly round the snow covered garden. "I'm looking for your stop-cock," he exclaimed.

"What!" bellowed Mr. Curry, putting a hand to his ear to make sure he'd heard aright. "Cock! How dare you call me cock! I shall report you to Mrs. Bird."

"I didn't mean you were to stop, cock," explained Paddington desperately. "I meant..."

"Stop?" repeated Mr. Curry. "I most certainly will not stop. What's going on? Where's Mr. James?"

"You're having trouble with your 'U' bends, Mr. Curry," cried Paddington.

"Round the bend!" spluttered Mr. Curry. "Did I hear you say I'm round the bend?"

Mr. Curry took a deep breath as he prepared to let forth on the subject of bears in general and Paddington in particular, but as he did so a strange look came over his face and before Paddington's astonished gaze he began dancing up and down, waving his arms in the air.

"Where's all this water coming from, bear?" he roared. "I've got ice cold water all over my feet. Where's it all coming from?"

But if Mr Curry was expecting an answer to his question he was unlucky for a second later the sound of another front door being slammed punctuated his remarks, only this time it was the one belonging to number thirty-two.

Paddington had been thinking for some while that he'd had enough of plumbing for one day and the expression on Mr. Curry's face quite decided him in the matter.

Mr. Brown looked up from his morning paper as a burst of hammering shook the dining-room. "I shall be glad when they've finished next door," he said. "They've been at it for days now. What on earth's going on?"

"I don't know," said Mrs. Brown, as she poured out the coffee. "Mr. Curry's got the builders in. I think it's something to do with his bathroom. He's been acting strangely all the week. He came round specially the other evening to give Paddington sixpence and several mornings he's sent the baker round with a bun."

"Mr. Curry gave Paddington *sixpence?*" echoed Mr. Brown, lowering his paper.

"I think he had a nasty accident during the cold weather," said Mrs. Bird. "He's having a complete new bathroom paid for by the insurance company."

"Trust Mr. Curry to get it done for nothing," said Mr. Brown. "Whenever I try to claim anything from my insurance company there's always a clause in small print at the bottom telling me I can't."

"Oh," said Mrs. Bird. "I have a feeling this was more of a *paws* than a *clause*. It's what Mr. Curry calls an 'act of bear'."

"An act of bear?" repeated Mr. Brown. "I've never heard of that one before."

"It's very rare," said Mrs. Bird. "Very rare indeed. In fact it's so rare I don't think we shall hear of it again, do you, Paddington?"

The Browns turned towards Paddington, or what little could be seen of him from behind a large jar of his special marmalade from the cut-price grocer in the market. But the only sound to greet them was that of crunching toast as he busied himself with his breakfast.

Paddington could be very hard of hearing when he chose. All the same, there was a look about him suggesting that Mrs. Bird was right and that as far as one member of the household was concerned bathrooms were safe from "acts of bear" for many winters to come.

CHAPTER TEN

Paddington and the Christmas Pantomime

"Harold Price?" said Mrs. Brown. "Wants to see me? But I don't know anyone called Harold Price, do I?"

"It's the young man from the big grocery store in the market," said Mrs. Bird. "He said it had something to do with their amateur dramatic society."

"You'd better show him in then," said Mrs. Brown. Now that Mrs. Bird mentioned it she did vaguely remember Harold Price. He was a rather spotty faced young man who served behind the jam counter. But for the life of her she couldn't imagine what that had to do with amateur dramatics.

"I'm so sorry to trouble you," said Mr. Price as Mrs. Bird ushered him in to the dining-room. "But I expect you

146

know there's a drama festival taking place in the hall round the corner this week."

"You'd like us to buy some tickets?" asked Mrs. Brown, reaching for her handbag.

Mr. Price shifted uneasily. "Well...er...no, not exactly," he said. "You see, we've entered a play for the last night — that's tomorrow — and we've been let down at the last moment by the man who was going to do the sound effects. I was told you have a young Mr. Brown who's very keen on that sort of thing but I'm afraid I've forgotten his Christian name."

"Jonathan?" asked Mrs. Brown.

Mr. Price shook his head. "No, it wasn't Jonathan," he said. "It was a funny sort of name. He's been on television."

"Not *Paddington?*" said Mrs. Bird.

"That's it!" exclaimed Mr. Price. "Paddington! I knew it was something unusual.

"I wrote this play myself," he continued eagerly. "It's a sort of mystery pantomime and we're hoping it may win a prize. The sound effects are most important and we must have someone reliable by tomorrow night."

"Have you ever met Paddington?" asked Mrs. Bird.

"Well, no," said Mr. Price. "But I'm sure he could do them, and if he'll come I can let you all have free seats in the front row."

"That's most kind of you," said Mrs. Brown. "I don't know what to say. Paddington does make rather a noise sometimes when he's doing things — but I don't know that you'd exactly call them sound effects."

"Please!" appealed Mr. Price. "There just isn't anyone else we can ask."

"Well," said Mrs. Brown doubtfully, as she paused at the door. "I'll ask him if you like — but he's upstairs doing his accounts at the moment and I'm not sure that he'll want to be disturbed."

Mr. Price looked somewhat taken aback when Mrs. Brown returned, closely followed by Paddington. "Oh!" he stammered. "I didn't realise you were a...that is...I...er...I expected someone much older."

"Oh, that's all right, Mr. Price," said Paddington cheerfully, as he held out his paw. "I'm nearly four. Bears' years are different."

"Er...quite," said Mr. Price. "I'm sure they are." He took hold of Paddington's outstretched paw rather gingerly. Mr. Price was a sensitive young man and there were one or two old marmalade stains he didn't like the look of, not to mention a quantity of red ink from the debit side of Paddington's accounts which somehow or other managed to transfer itself to his hand.

"You're sure you hadn't anything else planned?" he asked hopefully.

"Oh no," said Paddington. "Besides, I like theatres and I'm good at learning lines."

"Well, they're not actually *lines*, Paddington," said Mrs. Brown nervously. "They're noises."

"Noises?" exclaimed Paddington, looking most surprised. "I've never heard of a 'noises' play before."

Harold Price looked at him doubtfully. "Perhaps we could use you in some of the crowd scenes," he said. "We're a bit short of serfs."

"Serfs?" exclaimed Paddington.

"That's right," said Mr. Price. "All you have to do is come on and say 'Odds bodikins' every now and then."

"Odds bodikins?" repeated Paddington, looking more and more surprised.

"Yes," said Mr. Price, growing more enthusiastic at the idea. "And if you do it well I might even let you say 'Gadzooks' and 'Scurvy knave' as well."

"Perhaps you'd both like to go into it all down at the hall," said Mrs. Brown hastily, as she caught sight of the expression on Paddington's face.

"A very good idea," said Mr. Price. "We're just about to start a rehearsal. I can explain it as we go along."

"He did say it's a pantomime?" said Mrs. Bird, when she returned from letting Paddington and Mr. Price out.

"I think he did," replied Mrs. Brown.

"Hmm," said Mrs. Bird. "Well, if Paddington has a paw in it there'll be plenty of pantomime — you mark my words!"

"Here we are," said Mr. Price, as he showed Paddington through a door marked PRIVATE — ARTISTS ONLY. "I'll take you along and introduce you to the others."

Paddington blinked in the strong lights at the back of the stage and then sniffed. There was a nice smell of greasepaint and it reminded him of the previous time he had been behind the scenes in a theatre, but before he had time to investigate the matter he found himself standing in front of a tall, dark girl who was stretched out on a couch.

"Deirdre," said Mr. Price. "I'd like you to meet the young Mr. Brown I was telling you about. He's promised to lend a paw with the sound effects."

The dark girl raised herself on one elbow and stared at Paddington. "You didn't tell me he was a *bear*, Harold," she said.

"I didn't know myself...actually," said Mr. Price unhappily. "This is Miss Flint, my leading lady," he explained, turning to Paddington. "She's in bacon and eggs."

"How nice," said Paddington, raising his hat politely. "I should like to be in bacon and eggs myself."

"You look rather as if you have been," said Miss Flint, shuddering slightly as she sank back on to the couch. "I suppose the show *must* go on, Harold — but *really!*"

Mr. Price looked at Paddington again. "Perhaps you'd better come with me," he said hastily, as he led the way across the stage. "I'll show you what you have to do."

After giving Miss Flint a hard stare Paddington followed Mr. Price until they came to a small table in the wings. "This is where you'll be," said Mr. Price, picking up a large bundle of papers. "I've marked all the places in the script where there are any sound effects. All you have to do is bang some coconuts together whenever it says 'horses hooves', and there's a gramophone for when we have any music or thunder noises."

150

Paddington listened carefully while Mr. Price explained about the script and he examined the objects on the table with interest.

"It looks a bit difficult," he said, when Mr. Price had finished his explanations, "especially with paws. But I expect it will be all right."

"I hope so," said Mr. Price. He ran his hands nervously through his hair and gave Paddington a last worried look as he went back on to the stage to join the rest of the cast. "I do hope so. We've never had a bear doing the sound effects before."

Mr. Price wasn't the only one to feel uneasy at the thought of Paddington taking part in his play and by the time the following evening came round everyone in the Brown household was in a high state of excitement as they got ready for their outing. Mr. Price had been as good as his word and he'd not only given Paddington a number of tickets for the family, but he'd slipped in an extra one for Mr. Gruber as well, and even Mr. Curry had promised to put in an appearance.

Paddington went on ahead of the others as he had one or two last minute adjustments to make to his gramophone, but he was waiting at the door to greet them when they arrived just before the start of the performance. He was wearing a large rosette marked OFFICIAL in his hat and he looked most important as he led the way down the crowded aisle to some seats in the front row of the stalls, before disappearing through a small door at the side of the stage.

As the Browns settled down in their seats a roll of thunder shook the hall and Mrs. Brown looked up anxiously. "That's very odd," she exclaimed. "Thunder at this time of the year. It was just starting to snow when we came in."

"I expect that was Paddington testing his sound effects," said Jonathan knowledgeably. "He said he had quite a few claps to do."

"Well, I wish he'd turn the volume down a bit," said Mrs. Bird, turning her attention to the stage as the curtain began to rise. "That ceiling doesn't look too safe to me."

"I think someone must have forgotten to pay the electric light bill," whispered Mr. Brown as he adjusted his glasses and peered at the scene.

Mr. Price's play was called *The Mystery of Father Christmas and the Disappearing Plans* and according to the programme the action all took place one night in the hall of a deserted castle somewhere in Europe.

From where they were sitting the Browns not only found it difficult to see what was going on, but when their eyes did get accustomed to the gloom they found it even harder to understand what the play was about anyway.

Several times Father Christmas came through a secret panel in the wall holding a lighted candle in his hand, and each time he disappeared he was followed after a short interval by Mr. Price playing the part of a mysterious butler. If Father Christmas was acting strangely, Mr. Price's actions were even more peculiar. Sometimes he came on waving the secret plans with a triumphant expression on his face, and at other times he looked quite sinister as he shook an empty fist at the audience to the accompaniment of a roll of thunder.

Behind the scenes Paddington was kept very busy. Apart from the thunder, there were the coconut shells to be banged together whenever anyone approached the castle, not to mention clanking drawbridge noises and creaking sounds each time a door was opened.

In fact there was so much to do it took him all his time to follow the script let alone watch the action on the stage and he was quite surprised when he looked up suddenly in the middle of one of his thunder records and found it was the interval.

"Very good work, Mr. Brown," said Harold Price, as he came off the stage mopping his brow and stopped by Paddington's table. "I couldn't have done it better myself. I don't think you missed a single cue."

"Thank you very much," said Paddington, looking very

pleased with himself as he returned Mr. Price's thumbs-up sign with a wave of his paw.

Quite a lot of people had come and gone in the first half of Mr. Price's play and altogether he wasn't sorry to sit down for a while and rest his paws. In any case the serfs had to put in several appearances during the second act and he was anxious to practise his lines while he had the chance.

It was some minutes after he had settled himself underneath the table with the script and a jar of marmalade that he noticed an unusual amount of noise going on at the back of the stage. It seemed to have something to do with Harold Price having mislaid his secret plans. Several times his voice rose above the others saying he couldn't go on without them because a lot of his most important lines were written on the back. Paddington scrambled out hurriedly in order to investigate the matter but by the time he stood up everything had gone quiet again and order seemed to have been restored as the curtain went up for the second act.

Paddington was looking forward to the second half of Mr. Price's play and even though a lot of people were still creeping around behind the scenes with anxious expressions on their faces he soon forgot about it as Father Christmas made his entrance and approached Miss Flint's couch in the centre of the stage.

From the little that could be seen of him behind his beard, Father Christmas looked most unhappy as he addressed Miss Flint. "I had hoped to bring thee glad tidings," he cried, in ringing tones. "But alas, I am undone for *I have lost the secret plans!*"

"You've *what?*" exclaimed Miss Flint, jumping up from her couch in alarm. Miss Flint had spent the interval in her dressing room and she was as surprised as anyone to learn that the plans really were missing. "What have you done with them?" she hissed.

"I don't know," said Father Christmas in a loud whisper. "I think I must have put them down somewhere.

"Er...nice weather we've been having lately," he continued in a loud voice as he played for time. "Hast thou read any good books lately?"

From his position at the side of the stage Paddington looked even more surprised than Miss Flint at the sudden turn of events. Mr. Price had explained the play very carefully to him and he felt sure no mention had been made of any character called Tidings. Then there was the question of the cloak. Father Christmas appeared to be wearing his cloak in exactly the same way that he'd worn it all through the play and yet he'd definitely said something about it having come undone. Paddington consulted his script several times in case he'd made a mistake, but the more he looked at it the more confused he became.

It was as he turned round to the desk in order to play one of his thunder records just to be on the safe side that he received yet another surprise, for there, lying in front of

155

him was a dog-eared pile of papers with the words SECRET PLANS — PROPERTY OF HAROLD PRICE written in large letters across the front.

Paddington looked at the papers and then back at the stage. A nasty silence seemed to have come over the audience, and even Father Christmas and Miss Flint appeared to have run out of conversation as they stared at each other in embarrassment.

Coming to a decision Paddington picked up the secret plans and hurried on to the stage with a determined expression on his face. After raising his hat several times to the audience he waved in the direction of the Browns and Mr. Gruber and then turned towards the couch.

"Odds bodikins!" he cried, giving Father Christmas a hard stare. "I've come to do you up."

"You've come to do what?" repeated Father Christmas nervously, as he stood clutching the candle in one hand and the end of the couch in the other.

"I'm afraid I can't see anything about Glad Tidings in my script," continued Paddington. "But I've found your secret plans."

Paddington looked very pleased with himself as a burst of applause came from the audience. "Scurvy knave!" he exclaimed, making the most of his big moment. "Gadzooks! You left them under my coconuts!"

"I left them *where?*" said Father Christmas in a daze, as Paddington held out the plans and he exchanged them for the candle.

"Under my coconuts," said Paddington patiently. "I

think you must have put them there in the interval."

"Fancy leaving your plans under a bear's coconuts," hissed Miss Flint. "A fine spy you are!"

While Miss Flint was talking a glassy look came over Father Christmas. So much had gone wrong already that evening it didn't seem possible anything else could happen, but there was definitely a very odd odour coming from somewhere.

"Can you smell something burning?" he asked anxiously.

Miss Flint paused. "Good heavens!" she cried, hurriedly taking the candle away from Paddington. "It's your beard — it's on fire!"

"It's all right, Mr. Christmas, I'm coming," called Paddington as he climbed up on to the couch. "I think I must have held the wick too close by mistake."

A gasp of surprise went up from the audience as Paddington took hold of the beard and gave it a tug.

"Well I'm blowed," said a voice near the Browns, as the whiskers came away in Paddington's paws and revealed the perspiring face of Harold Price. "Fancy that! It was the butler all the time — disguised as Father Christmas!"

"What a clever idea," said a lady in the row behind. "Having him unmasked by a bear."

"A most unusual twist," agreed her companion.

"My play!" groaned Harold Price, collapsing into a chair and fanning himself with the secret plans as the curtain came down. "My masterpiece — ruined by a bear!"

"Nonsense!" exclaimed Miss Flint, coming to Paddington's rescue. "It wasn't Mr. Brown's fault. If you hadn't lost the plans in the first place all this would never have happened. Anyway," she concluded, "the audience seem to like it — just listen to them."

Mr. Price sat up. Now that Miss Flint mentioned it there did seem to be a lot of applause coming from the other side of the curtain. Several people were shouting "Author" and someone even appeared to be making a speech.

"I feel," said the judge, as they joined him on the stage, "we must congratulate Harold Price on his pantomime. It was undoubtedly the funniest play of the week."

"The *funniest*," began Mr. Price. "But it wasn't meant to be funny..."

The judge silenced him with a wave of his hand. "Not only was it the funniest, but it had the most unusual ending I've seen for many a day. That serf bear," he said, as he consulted a piece of paper in his hand, "his name doesn't seem to appear on the programme — but he played his part magnificently. Remarkable timing — the way he set light to your beard. One false move with his paw and the whole lot might have gone up in flames!

"I have no hesitation," he concluded, amid a long burst of applause from the audience, "in awarding the prize for the best play of the festival to Mr. Harold Price."

Harold Price looked rather confused as the applause died away and someone called out "Speech". "It's very kind of you all," he said, "and I'm most grateful. But I think I ought to mention that although I *wrote* the play, young Mr. Brown here had quite a large paw in the way it ended.

"I shouldn't be standing here now if it wasn't for him," he added, as he turned to Paddington amid another outburst of clapping, "and I wouldn't like to think he'd gone unrecognised."

"How kind of Mr. Price to give Paddington some of the credit," said Mrs. Brown later that evening as they made their way home through the snow. "I wonder what he meant when he said Paddington had a paw in the ending?"

"Knowing Paddington's paws," said Mrs. Bird, "I shudder to think."

Mr. Gruber and the Browns looked back at Paddington in the hope of getting some kind of an explanation but his head was buried deep in his duffle coat and he was much too busy picking his way in and out of their footprints to hear what was being said.

Paddington liked snow, but while they'd been in the theatre rather too much had fallen for his liking and he was looking forward to warming his paws in front of the fire at number thirty-two Windsor Gardens.

Apart from that, the sight of a Christmas tree in someone's window had just reminded him of the date and he was anxious to get home as quickly as possible so that he could hang up his stocking.

There were still several more days to go before the holiday but after watching Mr. Price's play that evening Paddington didn't want to take any chances, particularly over such an important matter as Father Christmas.